Waking
The
Dead

Jo Wolfe supernatural thriller

Book 4

Wendy Cartmell

ISBN: 9798692529701

By Wendy Cartmell

Sgt Major Crane crime thrillers
Deadly Steps
Deadly Nights
Deadly Honour
Deadly Lies
Deadly Widow
Hijack
Deadly Cut
Deadly Proof

Emma Harrison Mysteries
Past Judgement
Mortal Judgement
Joint Judgement

Crane and Anderson crime thrillers
Death Rites
Death Elements
Death Call
A Grave Death
A Cold Death

Supernatural Mysteries
Gamble with Death
Touching the Dead
Divining the Dead
Watching the Dead
Waking the Dead
Playing with the Dead

For Eddie,
Your support is invaluable.
Thank you!

Prologue

Jo felt instantly at home, albeit a feeling which was soured with guilt. She was walking through the stable block at Homecroft Farm, petting each horse as she passed. They nibbled at her fingers, blew into her hands, and neighed their welcome. A peace stole over her as she reached the last stall and the horse that would be her mount that day. Silver was a beautiful grey mare, who looked at Jo with interest, then nodded her head in pleasure as Jo entered the stable and slipping on a headcollar, led her outside. Once Silver was saddled and Jo kitted out, she climbed onto the horse's back

She'd not told her father, nor her partner in more ways than one, DS Eddie Byrd, about her visit as both would have tried to stop her. But she felt safe enough if a bit giddy to begin with. Jo liked Baz, who owned the stables, and they were just going out for a quiet walk along the beach. She'd been longing to go for a ride for months and surely a quiet hack would be okay? Jo didn't need to go galloping over the South Downs. Not anymore. Not after the accident.

With Baz leading the way, they walked the short path

to the beach where they led the horses into the shallows. After checking Jo was still alright, Baz broke into a trot along the length of the sandy beach, with Jo following her. When they reached the end they stopped, facing outward to the sea.

Jo had loosened the reins, when suddenly Silver reared up in panic. Gripping with her knees and leaning over Silver's neck, Jo managed to stay on. As Silver returned to standing on four legs, Jo took a better hold of the reins and looked out to sea.

The tumbling waves were foaming, and Jo wondered what had spooked Silver. Then she saw it.

Coming at her over the sea was a horse, rearing up on the foam. Its mane seemed part of the waves, its mouth was open, lips curled back to reveal rows of discoloured teeth, with wild staring eyes that seemed to look straight into Jo's soul. Hooves clawed the air as it rode the waves like a surfer. The swell grew and tumbled, then crashed onto the beach and the horse was swallowed up by the mist.

Jo had heard of the legends surrounding horses. She'd read up on them when she was a girl and was fascinated by all things horse. It could only be a Kelpie, a malevolent shape-changing aquatic spirit of Scottish legend.

But if that were true, what the hell was one doing in Pagham, down on the coast from Chichester?

CHAPTER 1

Colin was feeling pretty low. He and his girlfriend Claire had just broken up. Well, not just, actually a couple of months ago. But it still felt like it was only yesterday. The pain was still strong, and he was yearning for her as he walked along Pagham Beach towards the nature reserve, not knowing, nor caring, where he was, or where he was going.

His mum thought he was out with his mates. Mates! What mates? He'd given up everything and everyone for Claire. What a fool he was, as he was left alone and lonely. And Claire? Well she'd gone off with her new man, hadn't she? Colin had tried his hardest to find another partner, had already gone through umpteen women, but so far without any luck. Most of them turned out to be either airheads or as desperate as he was, and desperation was not a good look.

Once Claire had confessed her transgressions, there went their relationship and their modern rented flat in the heart of Chichester. And Colin? Well, he was back at home with his mum and dad. How embarrassing was that? Nearly 30 years old and living with his parents in Pagham. Pathetic.

Pagham lay Just down the coast from Bognor Regis,

and as his mum kept telling him, nearby were lovely walks on public footpaths within the nature reserve. But the beach front was home to nothing more than loads of closed and padlocked beach huts. Scintillating stuff.

Sitting on the beach, watching the sea lap against the stones, he realised the tide was coming in, and slowly and resolutely the water was rising to meet his feet. He scrambled up before he got wet and turned to walk back home. The moon was becoming increasingly covered by cloud and there was a chilly note to the gentle breeze that had become a light wind.

Walking back along the path, he decided that he would go for a drink with his team at work the next night. There was to be a 'thank you' piss-up organised by the partners to celebrate all the hard work on the client presentation which was due to take place the next morning. He wouldn't normally be seen dead at a 'work's do', but beggars couldn't be choosers and anyway it was the only option he had for a bit of entertainment on Friday night.

Turning for home, he saw her. A wistful looking young woman scanning the shoreline. He had no idea what she was looking for, or why, as there was nothing there. The water was black and singularly uninviting. No boats were inbound, or outbound for that matter. They were entirely alone.

'Can I help you?' he asked, revelling in his role of protector of lost maidens everywhere. 'Are you lost?'

'Yes,' she said. 'I'm trying to get back to Happy Days holiday village, but I appear to have lost my way. I can't remember if I should turn left or right.'

She had large, dark, soulful eyes that were rapidly filling with tears. Her very long and very dark hair looked a little tangled. It reminded him of dreadlocks, but on closer inspection they looked more akin to corkscrew curls. Caught up in them were little flowers in a variety of colours. At least he thought they were flowers but

4

couldn't really see in the gloom.

'If you face the shore, you need to go to your left.'

'Um, are you going that way? Only, well, I know it sounds stupid, but it's true, I'm afraid of the dark, you see.'

She turned to her left and immediately fell over. Her tears flowed freely. 'Oh, what an idiot. Now I've twisted my ankle.'

'Here,' Colin said, holding out a hand. 'Up you get, then lean on my arm and I'll get you back in one piece.'

'Why thank you kind sir,' she sniffed. 'You've no idea how appreciative of your assistance I am.'

He thought her language strange, rather archaic and flowery, but shrugged it off, not wanting anything to spoil the moment. He really did need some company and after all he had very little else to do with his time.

As they walked, they talked, telling each other all about themselves and their sad stories. There was a definite affinity between them, for she knew exactly how Colin felt, as she had been jilted at the altar.

Before he realised, they had strolled out of Pagham, past the holiday village and onward to the lagoon. But neither of them seemed to mind.

Sitting on two large stones, side by side, they watched the moonlight play over the water. They turned to each other at the same time and his heart did a summersault. She was incredibly beautiful with the moon lighting up her face. She was looking at him with such longing that he felt brave enough to kiss her. And she kissed him back. He couldn't believe it. Instantly he was enchanted by her. Lost. He never wanted to leave her. He was ensnared in her arms. Colin might be rejected by those on land but was welcomed with open arms by those who lived in the deep.

CHAPTER 2

It was the shock of waking to find herself submerged in icy cold water, that made Jo gasp. Which was a mistake. She desperately needed to get air into her lungs and to cough up the water she'd just inadvertently swallowed. But the sea had closed over her head and it was pitch black. No longer knowing which way was up or down, Jo fought against her rising panic, trying to calm herself. She looked around her, but all she could see was blackness and a few bubbles. That was all there was to show for her life, she realised. Just a few bubbles drifting in the ocean, soon to disperse and be no more. Just like her. Very shortly she would be no more and there wouldn't even be a body for her family to find. She had to fight. But she also had to remain calm. Needing to conserve her energy and what little oxygen remained in her lungs, Jo forced her muscles to relax and began drifting downward.

Downwards. That was it. Now all she needed to do was to go in the opposite direction. That's where the surface must be. She kicked, as best she could in her weakened state, but very little happened. Cold, hard dread tracked down her spine. She wasn't going to make it on her own. She needed help.

Jo felt pressure on her shoulders. She tried to spin around. What was that? Who was that? She was being pulled this way and that. Pummelled. Trampled. As she spun, more oxygen was lost. Something kicked her in the back. Then the kidneys. She was being beaten up in the water. But she couldn't see what it was. She swirled in the maelstrom. She couldn't see to fight back. It must be the Kelpie. Oh God. It had come for her. Jo opened her mouth and screamed.

Then everything went black.

'Jo! Jo! Wake up!'

As Jo burst out of the sea, she gulped in air and spluttered out water. Shaking and shivering she opened her eyes. Judith. Of course. Her guardian angel, for want of a better phrase. It had been nothing more than a nightmare.

'Are you sure?' Judith asked.

'What?'

'That it was only a nightmare.'

She frowned. 'Judith, what are you doing here? What time is it?'

Glancing at the clock on the bedside table she saw it was 3 am. 'It's the middle of the night,' she grumbled and pushed her wet hair off her face. She realised she was still shivering with cold and shock. Her tee-shirt was damp and clammy, so were her briefs, her skin, her hair. She felt the bedclothes. Wet. Realisation dawned. 'I'm soaking! How is that possible?'

'Nothing's impossible, Jo,' Judith said. 'You should know that by now. It's the Kelpie. Beware of the Kelpie…' As her voice faded, so did Judith, until Jo was left alone in her bedroom.

'Oh for fuck's sake,' she grumbled as she climbed out of bed and headed for the en-suite shower. But as she stood under the hot water, trying her best to control her shivering, she realised that was the second brush with the Kelpie she'd had in the space of a few weeks. If it hadn't been for Judith… Jo didn't want to finish that thought.

Had she really been in danger, though? Or was it all just a bad dream? But the pile of wet clothes on the floor belied the dream theory. Wrapping herself in a large fluffy towel she traipsed into the bedroom and once more felt the bed. Wet. What the hell was going on?

CHAPTER 3

'You ready to go, Flo?'

Florence's husband shouted from the hall, just as she was collecting her handbag from the bedroom. 'On my way, love,' she replied and started to walk down the stairs.

Flo and her husband, Del, were off to a day out at Gunwharf Quays, an outlet shopping centre in Portsmouth and this outing was one she'd been looking forward to for weeks. She had on comfortable shoes, trousers and a long blouse that covered up her bumps and lumps. Her small umbrella was stowed safely in her handbag, even though the weather forecast was for sunshine, because you never could trust the English weather. Her lightweight jacket was draped over her arm. After taking one last look in the mirror and patting down her grey hair, which was streaked with silver and white, she walked down the stairs. And stopped at the bottom.

The house phone was ringing, which was an unusual occurrence. Normally everyone used their mobiles. Flo considered letting it ring, it was probably some scammer wanting money. But it kept ringing. Didn't stop. She began to consider it a portent for disaster. Who on earth was it? What was wrong?

'Come on, Flo!' her husband shouted, but she ignored him.

Flo shivered as she reached for the handset.

'Mrs Deed?' a voice said before Flo could say anything. 'Oh, thank goodness I've managed to reach you. It's Cooper from CCP Design, it's about Colin.'

'Wh, wh, what about him?' Flo's knees refused to take her weight and she collapsed on the stairs with a thump.

'It's just that he's not here... and we've got a presentation to a new client... they're due in an hour and he's not here!' Cooper's voice was rising in pitch and volume.

'What do you mean he's not there?' It didn't compute. Colin was fastidious about his design work. He'd not had a sick day in over two years. He'd been excited about the forthcoming presentation, surely he'd never miss it.

'He didn't turn up this morning. Is he there?'

Flo looked at her watch. It was 10 am. 'Hang on,' she mumbled and put the phone down on the floor. Stumbling up the stairs she reached the top, tripping over the last step and skidding to a halt at Colin's bedroom door. Grabbing the handle she pulled herself up, then pushed open the door.

The room was empty. The bed not slept in.

Where the hell was he?

Del appeared behind her. 'Flo? What's the matter? Who is that on the phone?'

He put his hands on her shoulders, but it didn't stop the shivering. 'It's Colin. He's not at work. And he's not here. Look, his bed's not been slept in. Did you see him this morning?' Flo asked as she turned to her husband.

Flo held her breath, wishing, hoping, needing Del to say yes. But he didn't.

'No, I thought he'd left for work early, he's that thingy today hasn't he?'

Flo managed to nod, then took a deep breath and

10

cleared her throat before saying, 'Yes he has. But I didn't see him this morning either. I thought the same as you.' A further thought struck Flo. 'Did you see him, or perhaps heard him come in last night?'

She could see the look of dawning horror on her husband's face. He shook his head and pulled her to him. He stroked her hair and then kissed the top of her head. But it didn't help. A coldness was seeping through Flo's bones. She doubted she'd ever be warm again.

CHAPTER 4

'Morning, Jed,' DI Jo Wolfe called as she entered Chichester police station, returning from a meeting with the Forensic Laboratory.

Jed was the desk sergeant for the day shift, a competent yet empathetic officer who ruled the entrance to the station with an iron rod, but never forgot that he was dealing with human beings.

Jed raised his hand in greeting and spoke. But not to Jo. Into the telephone receiver he was holding he said, 'Yes, I know, madam... I understand your...please try and stay calm... a day or so, yes that's what I said.'

Jo could hear the squawking from the telephone from where she stood. She frowned at Jed and he mouthed, 'Help!'.

Jo nodded and let herself into the area behind the reception desk.

'Madam, please, yes a senior officer is here, DI Wolfe, let me just speak to her for you.'

Jed pressed a button and blew out his breath. 'I've got a Mrs Florence Deed on the line,' Jed told Jo. 'She rang the station direct. Her son's missing, hasn't been seen since yesterday.'

'A child?' Jo knew that was every parent's nightmare and her heart sank.

'No, a 29-year-old male. I've tried to tell her its normal to wait a little while with a missing adult who is absent without any immediate cause for concern, and to give him time to turn up, but she's adamant this is unusual behaviour. I don't have any uniforms spare at the moment, there's that big fire up on the industrial estate and it's all hands to the pump up there.'

Jo took a moment to calculate in her head her current open cases. There was nothing that couldn't wait, and this sounded intriguing. 'Get her address and tell her I'll go to see her straight away.'

Jed nodded and Jo pulled out her mobile to tell Byrd to meet her in reception.

'And we're doing this because?'

Byrd's scepticism wasn't lost on Jo. 'Because she's a mother and desperately worried about her son, and there's no one else to go,' she insisted. Why did everyone think there was an ulterior motive when Jo wanted to do something?

He flung her a look, then went back to driving.

Jo tried to make her face expressionless. But Byrd knew her too well. And he mustn't know about the riding and the Kelpie. But Jo had a horrible feeling that the two events could be about to collide – seeing the Kelpie and a young man going missing. Jo shivered despite the heat in the car.

As they drove towards Pagham, along the road out of Bognor Regis, the area became quieter. Less people. Less cars. And then on the water, less boats, less activity. When they arrived at the village the only sound was the haunting call of the seagulls.

Byrd parked outside a well-tended dormer bungalow, fronted by a driveway leading to a garage. Bay trees stood either side of the front door, under a sloping tiled roof that formed a porch. A man Jo put in his mid-60's answered their knock. He had swept back mousy hair, but plenty of it, just beginning to thin at the sides. He had on non-descript grey trousers, held up by a black belt across his podgy middle, and a grey shirt.

Byrd introduced them and they both held up their identification. He gave them a wan smile and showed them into a living room, which ran the length of the house. The furniture had a tendency towards fussy and sat on a yellow cloth sofa was a woman, scrunching a handkerchief in her hands. She looked up with red eyes and realising who was calling, she rose and said, 'Is there any news? Have you found him yet?'

'Mrs Deed,' Jo said, 'I'm DI Wolfe and this is DS Byrd. If you remember I was there when you rang the station this morning.'

'Yes, yes, of course,' she said, 'please call me Flo,' and sat back down again. Then she stood, 'Would you like tea, coffee, anything?'

'Perhaps your husband would get us a drink,' Jo said. 'DS Byrd knows what we like,' and Jo indicated that Eddie should leave them alone. Jo sat on the edge of the sofa, nearest to Mrs Deed and said, 'Can you tell me what's happened?'

Mrs Deed nodded, her hair not shifting as she moved her head. But all the same Mrs Deed touched it, as if puffing it up at the sides and back. A nervous habit decided Jo.

'We were just about to leave for a day out in Portsmouth when the phone rang. It was Colin's firm, CCP Design in Chichester, asking if we knew where he was. He was needed urgently at work for a client presentation and they didn't understand why he wasn't there. At once I knew there was something wrong.' Mrs Deed paused while she wiped tears from her face.

'And why was that?'

'Because Colin is meticulous when it comes to work. He is never late, works extra if the need arises and had been practicing for this presentation all week.'

'What do CCP Design do?'

Again the hesitation while Mrs Deed wiped her face. She took a shaky breath. 'They're an advertising agency. They plan all sorts of campaigns from newspapers and magazines to television.'

Jo smiled. 'You seem to know a lot about it.'

'Well, yes, I like to take an interest. Wouldn't you?' Flo's brow furrowed in disbelief.

'Of course, it's what any good mother would do,' Jo soothed and was relieved when it seemed to do the trick and Mrs Deed relaxed. 'When did you last see Colin?'

'Last night. He was meeting a friend for a drink. He said he wouldn't be late, but not to wait up. So, so I didn't. I wished I had now.'

Jo glanced out of the window but couldn't see any cars parked in the road. 'Does he have a car? Has it gone?'

'He doesn't have one, never really needed it. He lived in central Chichester, you see.'

Jo didn't see, but let it slide for now as Byrd came back into the room with Mr Deed. 'Thanks for all that information, Mr Deed, that will be a big help.'

That was Jo's cue. She took a drink from one of the glasses of water for her and Byrd and then stood. 'We'd better be getting back to the station,' she said to Flo.

'What? Why?' Flo looked aghast and grabbed for her husband's hand.

'Because I'm sure Mr Deed has given us a lot of information on Colin that will help a great deal.'

Jo was careful not to upset Mrs Deed further by telling her that they should give Colin a chance to return home of his own free will. Either that or there needed to be strong evidence to suggest that something criminal had befallen him.

'So what we need you to do, is to contact his work colleagues and friends to see if they've seen him. Are there any family members he might have been in touch with? We need for you to list them all out with their contact details and information about the last time they saw, or spoke, to Colin. Could you do that for us? It really would be a great help.'

Flo Deed nodded and once more wiped her eyes. But she didn't look convinced that the strategy would help any.

CHAPTER 5

Del closed the door behind the police and returned to the living room and his wife, who had been watching the police leave through the net curtain.

'What do you think, Del? I don't think they believed me. But I know something's wrong, dreadfully wrong.' Flo's voice was rising in pitch and volume.

'Now, now,' Del grabbed his wife's hand. 'Don't go upsetting yourself.'

Flo sat down on the sofa and Del joined her. 'I can feel it, you know. He's in danger. This is so out of character. Oh, if only his relationship hadn't broken down. If that tart hadn't left him and run off with someone else, we wouldn't be in this nightmare.'

'Look, Flo, you can't go around speculating about things you know nothing about.'

'So what shall I do? I've got to do something!'

'Do what they said. Make lists of the people Colin knows and put down their contact details if you know them.'

'I think I've got some numbers in my phone.'

'Exactly, let's do all we can to help the police find him. Let's pull everything together and then you can start ringing round.'

Flo nodded.

'I tell you what, you go and wash that face of yours, your make up is running and I'll make us a nice coffee. These have gone cold. How about that, eh?'

Flo nodded and taking a shaky breath, stood, and walked to the stairs. Then she turned and said, 'We will find him, won't we, Del?'

'Of course we will, now off you go.'

Flo nodded and started to climb the stairs. Del moved to the kitchen, but once there didn't turn on the kettle, but grabbed the work surface to stop himself falling over. Despite all the positive things he'd said to Flo, he had the awful feeling that they'd never see their son again. But he daren't mention that. He needed to keep such thoughts to himself and do all he could to bolster Flo. But it was going to be tough. Very tough.

CHAPTER 6

Flo found that Del's advice worked. While she was on the phone trying to find Colin, her emotions were pushed to the back of her conscious mind. But after a while all the negative answers she was receiving got to her.

When she rang his office for the third time, the receptionist answered a mournful, 'No,' to Flo's query if Colin had turned up there yet.

Several people were calling her back and she found herself looking at her phone with laser focused eyes, as though she could make Colin ring her just by the sheer thought of him. When the phone did ring, she jumped and fumbled at the handset nearly cutting the call off.

She managed a querulous, 'Hello?' hoping to God it was Colin. But it wasn't.

'Hi, Aunty Flo, it's Ryan. I saw loads of missed calls from you on my mobile. Are you and Uncle Del alright? What's happened?'

Flo realised she had alarmed her nephew and apologised. 'I'm sorry, Ryan, it's just that I can't find Colin and wondered if you'd spoken to him recently?'

'Can't find him? What's he been up to now?'

'I've no idea, Ryan. Please answer my question.'

There was a brief pause, before Ryan said, 'I've not seen him for a while now, Aunty Flo.'

'Not seen him? How is that possible? You're his best friend!'

Flo could feel coldness running down her neck and spine.

'I'm sure he'd told me he was going out for a drink with you last weekend.'

'Oh dear. He might have told you that, but...' Ryan paused, which Flo took to be ominous. 'Well it's just not true.'

'It's not?'

'Aunty Flo, I haven't seen Colin since he broke up with Claire, a couple of months ago now.'

Flo clasped a hand over her mouth. She was afraid she was going to be sick. Dread filled her. What the hell was going on? What hadn't Colin been telling them?

Choking back a sob, she threw the phone onto the table and bolted for the stairs, ignoring the shouts coming from the handset and Del's questioning look.

She stumbled on the first stair and was forced to put out her hands on the treads and climbed crab-like to the top. Reaching the sanctuary of her bedroom she slammed the door behind her.

Suddenly it was real. Colin was missing. She had no idea where he was, or even what he'd been up to since he'd moved back home. It was as though the reality that she'd relied on was nothing more than smoke and mirrors. It seemed he was a different person than the son she knew. How had they drifted so far apart that he felt he couldn't confide in her anymore?

Flo didn't want her son to be a 'mummy's boy' but she'd always made a point of talking to Colin, discussing his work and what she thought were his leisure pursuits and interests. How could she have got it so wrong?

The sobs that had been threatening finally spewed out

of her mouth and she buried her head in the pillow and released a storm of tears that she couldn't keep at bay any longer.

CHAPTER 7

The next day Jo and Byrd were at the Deed's house once again. The mood was sombre, despair hanging heavily in the air. Colin still hadn't been found and was now officially missing.

'I'm so sorry, Mrs Deed,' said Jo. 'But rest assured we'll do all we can to try and trace Colin.'

Florence Deed nodded. She seemed to be dressed in the same clothes she had on yesterday. She had a scrunched-up handkerchief in her hand, which was pressed to her mouth. Her face was pinched and pale, and red rimmed eyes stood out starkly against her white skin.

'Do you have the list we asked for?' said Byrd.

'Aye,' said Del Deed. 'Here,' and he handed Byrd a handwritten sheet, who passed it to Jo.

Glancing at it she said, 'Thank you, this looks very comprehensive. We also need a recent photograph if you have one?'

Del and Flo both nodded. 'On our phones, like,' said Del.

'That's fine, you have my mobile number you can send me one through.'

'On that WhatsApp thingy?'

'Yes,' Jo smiled. 'On that.'

Del nodded but didn't return the smile. Both Mr and Mrs Deed looked shellshocked. And with good reason. Two days ago they were a happy family. And now? Now Jo didn't know if they'd survive a protracted missing person case. They were already acting as though they had nothing to live for anymore.

'We will do our absolute best to find Colin. You do know that?'

They both nodded, but neither seemed capable of speech. Jo didn't know what else to say to them. Words were cheap. But the right words? Well, they were like gold dust.

'Can we see his room, please? asked Byrd.

'Of course,' said Del. 'The first door at the top of the stairs.'

Jo and Eddie climbed the stairs silently, the thick wool carpet underfoot deadening any noise. They both pulled on gloves and Eddie pushed the door, which creaked as it opened to reveal a large bedroom facing the street. They went in and Byrd closed the door behind them.

'What's that for?' said Jo.

'So you can do your thing. You know, touch stuff. It might tell you where he is.'

'I'm not a performing seal!' admonished Jo. 'I can't do it to order.' For a moment she wished Byrd didn't know about her visions, she didn't like being under the microscope. If an inanimate object had something to tell her, it would. But she couldn't make it. Nor could she summon up information, just because she needed it. 'Let's just get on with looking, shall we?'

'You're the boss,' Eddie said and opened a large, dark wood wardrobe.

As he was flicking through the clothes, Jo turned her attention to the bed. On one of the bedside tables stood three items. A lamp, a clock, and a black leather rectangular case. Jo picked it up. As she opened it, she found it was a Kindle. Sitting down on the bed she turned the device on.

But she'd turned on more than the Kindle. Instead of a page of the book Colin was reading, she saw a picture of him on the screen. It was night. He was sat on what looked like the edge of a pebble beach, bathed in subdued lighting from a nearby lamp post. He was looking out to sea. The moonlight glistened on the dark waters. He had his legs bent at the knee, with his elbows resting on them and literally his head in his hands. Jo could feel the melancholy emanating from him. He shook his head. He was a man who couldn't summon up a reason for living anymore. Jo watched in horror as he stood, and she knew for certain that he intended to walk into the sea. As he scrunched over the pebbles, a voice called to him. He turned to see a young woman. She appeared to be asking Colin for help. To Jo's utter relief he walked back up the beach towards her...

Jo jumped as the Kindle fell to the floor, startling her out of the vision.

'Are you okay?' Byrd called; his voice muffled by the clothes he was examining deep in the wardrobe.

'What? Oh, yes, just dropped something that's all.' She picked up the now closed Kindle and shaking an evidence packet out of her pocket, put it in. Standing and turning her attention to the bed she felt all over the top of it, then picked up each pillow in turn, flattening them to see if there was anything hidden in there. She came up a blank, so got down on her knees and put her hands under the mattress, feeling along the top of the divan base. That was where she used to put things she wanted hidden from her dad. But there was nothing. Did Colin not have any secrets from his parents? Or were they hidden elsewhere? Two of the many questions the missing person enquiry was certain to throw up as it progressed.

Jo and Byrd completed their rudimentary search of the room, but didn't find anything else of interest, other than Colin's laptop and his hairbrush with several hairs caught in its bristles. They took their haul downstairs and Byrd went to put them in the car, while Jo explained to Mr and Mrs Deed what they'd done.

'We've found some things that may be of interest,' she said. 'Just his Kindle and stuff. Things that might help us get to know Colin a little better. That includes his laptop,' she said. 'I've lifted the lid, but it needs a pin number. I don't suppose you know what that is?'

Flo shook her head, but Del nodded saying, 'Aye, I do.'

His wife looked at him in astonishment.

'Colin phoned from work one day to say he'd left his laptop at home by mistake. He needed some information from it, so asked me to go upstairs and look for him. That's how I know.'

'Where was I?'

It seemed Flo didn't like being left out of any corner of Colin's life and Jo wondered if Colin had felt claustrophobic living back at home with his parents.

'I dunno. Shopping or something I expect.'

Jo quickly asked, 'What is it Mr Deed?'

'What?' Del tore his focus away from his wife.

'His pin number?'

'Sorry, it's 2707.'

'That's his birthday!' said a stricken Flo and burst into tears.

While Del was comforting his wife, Jo mumbled something about being in touch as soon as possible and beat a hasty retreat, eager to get back to the office. But first there was a location she needed to visit.

CHAPTER 8

'Right, Boss,' said Eddie, starting the car. 'Back to the ranch?'

'Mmm,' said Jo. 'But via the beach.'

'What? Fancy an ice cream, do you?'

Jo threw him a look.

'Sorry,' he grinned, 'but you did walk into that one.'

Within a few hundred yards, Byrd stopped the car, parking alongside the road that ran parallel to the beach. It struck Jo just how near to the sea the Deed's home was.

'You could walk this in a few minutes,' she said climbing out of the car. There was a cold wind coming off the sea and she pulled the edges of her trouser suit jacket together and buttoned it up. In the distance, she could see dark clouds gathering and a stiffening breeze ruffled the unruly curls of her short dark hair.

'Do you think this is where he came then?' asked Byrd, walking around the car to her. He was wearing his own 'uniform' of brogues with skinny fitting trousers and a v neck pullover with a shirt underneath it. 'Oh God, do you think he's committed suicide?'

'To be honest, Byrd, I'm not sure. Let's see what we can get from his laptop and his emails. It may give a good indication as to his state of mind. Flo did think he was still upset about the breakdown of his relationship.'

'Yeah, but to kill yourself over a woman?' Byrd shuddered.

'Oh, so you wouldn't care if I chucked you then?' Jo teased.

'That's not what I meant, and you know it.'

She smiled, 'Sorry, I was just being flippant,' and she slipped her arm through his and kissed his cheek.

'That's better,' he said. 'But I think I need one on the other cheek.'

Jo happily obliged.

'And on the lips too,' he said, pouting.

'Bugger off,' she said smiling and turned to look out to sea.

They were roughly where Jo had seen Colin sitting on the beach in her vision. She looked up and down the road and sure enough there were lamp posts lining the path. Opposite the beach stood a row of houses, with the odd bed and breakfast dotted amongst them. Maybe uniformed officers could locate some cameras from them that covered the beach. Even partial cover would be a good start.

Jo turned over in her mind her To Do list. It was getting longer every minute.

'Come on, Byrd, we best get back,' she said and began to mentally plot her strategy as they took the road back to Chichester.

CHAPTER 9

Once back at the station Jo had no option but to see DCI Sykes. Not her favourite boss. Sykes seemed out to get her and after her last case her dad had confessed that Sykes had tried to pump him for information about Jo. That wasn't something Jo had wanted to hear, but, as her dad had said, she needed to. It was imperative she watched her back if she wanted to keep her job.

Never before had a superior officer made her feel undermined, but Sykes had turned it into an art form. So, even though she was the senior investigating officer on call when the case broke, she still needed to confirm with Sykes that it was her investigation and that she could continue with it.

Sykes was dealing with paperwork when she stopped outside his office. His head was bowed, and he hadn't seemed to sense her presence. She knocked lightly on the open door. 'Boss?'

He huffed before he lifted his head. 'Yes, Jo?' The boredom in his voice was not a good start. He must be having a bad day. Whether or not that was anything to do with Jo was an unknown quantity.

'The new case I caught yesterday -'

'Yes?' he interrupted.

'It has turned into a missing person enquiry.'

'You sure about that?' His eyes narrowed as he stared at her. 'Have you done a risk assessment?'

'Yes, Sir.' Jo was determined not to be intimidated. 'His disappearance is completely out of character and there was an important client presentation at work yesterday that he should have attended.'

'Hmm,' Sykes chewed the top of his pen deep in thought.

Even though he would have to have a bloody good reason for not letting Jo have the case, which she didn't think he had, she was unable to read him.

'He was very diligent and conscientious about his work and everyone is insisting something must have happened to him,' she continued.

Sykes sighed. 'Like what?'

Jo was taken aback at Sykes' attitude. It was as if Jo was boring him. She was talking about a human being for God's sake! 'Maybe he's had an accident, been taken, or worst-case scenario, been murdered?'

Sykes carried on chewing his pen, then took it out of his mouth and placed it on his desk. 'Oh alright. But keep me updated. Dismissed.'

Jo was rooted to the spot. Dismissed? She wasn't in the bloody army. As Sykes bent his head once again to his paperwork, Jo remembered to walk away. Unbelievable. Sykes either didn't care that a young man was missing or didn't care what Jo got up to. Either way, he'd make sure that any mistakes were laid squarely on her shoulders. She resolved not to give him the satisfaction and hurried down the stairs to her team.

She was gratified to find that they were already waiting for her, lounging near a white board that had a photograph of Colin Deed top and centre, with a family tree, more photographs, and a large-scale local area map.

'Thanks for this, Byrd,' Jo acknowledged his work and he nodded briefly back.

'So, Colin Deed, was last seen two nights ago leaving the family home in Pagham, here.' Jo pointed to the location of the bungalow on the map. 'Byrd and I have been to see his parents, Mr and Mrs Deed this morning. Jill, I'd like you to act as point of contact for them on this one.'

'Yes, Guv,' Jill said.

'It will be good experience for you,' Jo finished as Jill nodded her agreement. 'As the case unfolds it might be necessary to give them their own family liaison officer, but we'll keep that under review. Sasha? We need to find Colin's mobile phone. We have the number and his provider from his parents, detailed here. Get onto them and get access to his calls and texts. Can we also find out the last tower it pinged? You've also got his laptop and his pin number.'

Sasha nodded and bent her head to write down the information from the whiteboard.

'Colin stayed out overnight and hasn't been seen since. He's had no contact with anyone since that time, as far as we are aware,' said Jo.

'What do you think has happened to him?' asked Ken.

Jo shook her head. 'Worst case scenario? Murdered by person or persons as yet unknown. Or he's lying injured somewhere; had an accident; been arrested; or just decided he needed some time out to himself and his thoughts. It mustn't have been easy returning home to live with your parents at nearly 30. I need you to check all our cameras around Pagham and see if you can find him the night he went missing. I've got uniforms going up and down the nearby streets to see if anyone saw anything that night.'

Byrd said, 'Jill, can you confirm if Colin has taken his passport. If he has can you let the ports and airports know please, he may decide to leave the country, or have already left.'

'Do you think we need specialist officers or resources, such as the force helicopters, or dogs, Guv?' asked Ken.

'That's a tough one,' said Jo. 'I've no evidence to indicate Colin is a 'vulnerable person' nor any evidence of a crime having been committed against him. Let's hold back on that for now. Sasha can you circulate details on our local information systems and to relevant local partners, hospitals, ambulance service, taxi and bus firms and the like.'

'What is Colin like?' asked Jill and Jo was glad to hear her refer to him in the present tense. They were a long way from a murder enquiry yet.

Byrd spoke. 'Good son, good employee, but upset since the breakup of his relationship. His parents are insisting that there is no way he would have been away this long and not told them. But to be fair they don't really know if that would be the case or not. He's only been back with them for a couple of months. Who knows what he used to get up to in Chichester?'

'To that end, Byrd and I are going to interview his ex-partner,' Jo pointed to the picture of a young woman on the board, 'and his cousin Ryan, who his parents said is Colin's best friend. Let's reconvene at 4pm this afternoon and see if we're any further forward.'

'Boss.'

'Guv.'

The small core band of Jo's team all moved away back to their desks. As she watched them bend over their tasks by phone and computer, Jo hoped she would be able to keep her team around her. Her very own band of brothers. Sykes might be going for her personally, but she'd fight hard to keep him away from her team. She could only hope she was strong enough to defeat Sykes. And strong enough to defeat who, or what, had taken Colin.

CHAPTER 10

Ryan Deed seemed to bounce into the interview room. He was Colin's cousin on his father's side, and you could see the family resemblance in the two. Del and his brother Frank were twins, which meant that their sons were very alike. Both had the same nose, mouth, and jutting chin. It was all a bit disconcerting, Jo decided as she stood when Byrd and Ryan entered the room.

'Thanks for coming,' Jo said to Ryan as Byrd and he settled in their chairs. 'We'd appreciate your input as someone who knows Colin well, on a personal level.'

'I don't know what to say,' Ryan ran his hands through his hair, indicating his worry for his cousin. 'This going missing stuff. It's so unlike him.'

'What was his state of mind when you last saw him?' asked Byrd.

'Oh, you know, up and down. But he was doing his best to enjoy life as a single man, if you get my meaning.'

'No,' said Byrd. 'Sorry we don't.'

'Well, the girls.'

'Girls?'

Ryan turned to look at Jo. 'Yes, girls. On FANCY. You know, a little bit of what you fancy and all that.'

'Oh, online dating?'

Ryan spluttered. 'It's more like online shagging if you ask me.'

'Really?'

'Yeah. You know, you post where you are and see who else is available in your area.'

'In your town, do you mean?'

'Yes, but at times you can get people within a few hundred yards of you. In the same pub, or another one close by. If they are also single and available, well not necessarily single but available, and if you fancy their looks, you can meet up. Easy peasy.'

'Then they would have sex?' clarified Byrd.

'Yeah, after a drink or two, that's the general idea.'

Suddenly Jo felt old. Thank God she had Byrd. It sounded like a harsh world out there in singles land. 'Is that what Colin did? Meet people on the spur of the moment?'

'I reckon so.'

'Why do you think that?'

'Because he's done it before.'

'How many times?'

'Lots actually. It's his MO for want of a better phrase.'

'Do his parents know?'

'Dear God, no,' Ryan laughed at Jo's suggestion. 'They think he lives the life of a monk. They are very conservative people who don't even believe in sex before marriage. I guess they have outdated morals. They hadn't really approved of Colin and Claire living together. Anyway, whatever Colin's reasons for doing it, it is what it is. I didn't criticise him for doing it. Who am I to judge anybody?'

'What do you think were his reasons, though?' Byrd probed.

'Look, he'd just been dumped big time. I reckon it was a bit of a backlash from that. Flexing his single muscles.'

'Was he upset about the breakup?'

'Oh yes, he tried to hide it, but it was always there, you know. Under the surface, affecting everything he thought and did.'

'Enough to commit suicide?'

Ryan paused and thought. Then shook his head. 'No, on balance I'd say no he wouldn't.' Then Ryan grinned. 'Let's face it he was having too much fun.'

CHAPTER 11

Once Ryan had gone, it was time to Interview Colin's ex-girlfriend Claire. She'd responded to their telephone request to come in and give them some background on him. Jo wanted to see Claire for herself. They'd be better able to tell if she was lying in a face to face interview.

'Thanks for coming, Claire,' Jo said as she stood when Byrd ushered her into the room. Jo hadn't been sure what to expect but this short woman in front of her wasn't really it. She had on high heels but to be honest they didn't help much. She had long blond hair which fell in soft curls around a heart-shaped face. She was wearing a smart dress as though she had come directly from work.

The first thing Claire said was, 'You think Colin's missing?'

'Yes, I'm afraid he is. Which seems to be entirely out of character.'

Claire nodded, looking nonplussed but didn't comment. Jo decided it was as though Claire was trying hard not to be affected by Colin's strange behaviour. And failing.

'What was your relationship with him like?' Byrd said as he opened his notebook.

'How do you mean?' Claire looked from one to the other. For the first time she was looking nervous.

'Oh, you know, was he nice, kind, violent, moody? And why did you split up?'

'I found someone else, that's all.' She looked down at her hands.

'Why? Were you looking for a new man?'

'No, it was just one of those things, you know. It just happened.'

'So no other reason than that for dumping Colin?' Jo was deliberately harsh.

'No, not really.'

But Jo thought Claire was looking uncomfortable. She was fidgeting and her eyes kept darting all over the room.

'How was he? What was he like?' Jo pressed, doing a fair job of fidgeting herself as she tried to get comfortable on the unforgiving plastic chair.

'Pretty boring, actually.'

'Do you think he'd deliberately disappear?' asked Byrd.

'No why would he?'

'Any chance you think he might commit suicide? We understand he was pretty cut up about the end of your relationship.'

'No, surely not.' Claire's voice rose in volume and she pushed her hair off her face. 'I can't be responsible for that! I just can't! You haven't found him dead have you? Is that what this is all about? I can't bear it,' and she put her hands over her face and started crying.

'No one's saying it's your fault,' Jo reached across the table and grasped Claire's arm to comfort her.

At once she heard and saw their rows. Loud voices, horrible words, crashing of crockery. Colin criticising her for going out with her girlfriends. Convinced she was finding new men. Claire's tears and protestations that she wasn't. The threat of violence hanging heavy in the air.

But then she did meet someone. A friend from work. And that's when the sunshine came back into Claire's life. Able to smile again, allowed to be who she really was and not someone that Colin wanted her to be. Wanted to turn her into. The secretive packing of suitcases kept hidden under the bed. Calling in sick to work one day and waiting and praying for Colin firstly to go off to work and secondly not to come back. Once she was sure the coast was clear, she then took her cases to the car in the underground car park. Filled the boot with her stuff. And fled.

As the vision faded Jo stood. 'Thank you so much for coming in, Claire. If you do hear from Colin…'

Claire nodded and brushed her tears away. 'I'll let you know. But to be honest I hope I don't hear from him. He's not been very nice about the breakup.'

Jo walked Claire out to the front of the police station. As Claire went through the door, she looked up and saw a man and with tears flowing once more, she ran into his arms. Jo smiled at the protective gestures by Claire's new man, as the couple hugged and then left hand in hand.

'Well?' said Byrd when she returned from escorting Claire to the exit. 'What did you see? What was their relationship really like?'

Jo bit the denying retort back. Of course Byrd knew about her gift, she must try and remember that, but she had spent so long hiding her visions from her friends and family, it was a hard habit to break.

'Rows, criticism, controlling behaviour.'

'From Colin?'

Jo nodded.

'Violence?'

'Anger and jealousy definitely, with the threat of violence.'

Byrd sighed and collected their files from the table. 'Do you think she could have killed him?'

'No, I very much doubt it. She'd found happiness with her new man. There's no way she'd jeopardise that. But it's becoming clear that Colin isn't the whiter than white son his parents think he is.'

'The question is,' Byrd said. 'How much do we tell them?'

But Jo didn't have an answer to that one.

CHAPTER 12

As Jo and Byrd walked back into Major Crimes, Jo called, 'Right people, please tell me someone's got good news for me?'

'No luck with the interviews then, Guv?' Ken asked brushing cake crumbs from his jacket.

'Not so you'd notice, no,' Jo said, perching on the corner of Byrd's desk.

'Good job we've got something for you then,' and Ken winked at Sasha.

'Really? Sasha?'

Sasha had been studiously ignoring the interruption but sighed and lifting her eyes from her screen said, 'We've found Colin on a lone CCTV camera.'

'Bloody hell,' said Byrd. 'Well done you two.'

'Strictly speaking it was Ken who found it.'

'But you who cleaned the images up,' said a gallant Ken, which had absolutely no effect on Sasha at all. Not a smile. Not a flicker of an expression.

'Here,' she said, and an image appeared on the television next to their white boards. 'This was taken from a lone camera on one of the beach huts lining the shore.'

'There had been a spate of vandalism, so the owner set

up his own webcam,' explained Ken.

'Pretty low-resolution stuff, but I've cleaned it the best I can.'

Byrd peered at the screen. 'There's nothing there, just a path and some pebbles.'

'Wait a minute…there,' Sasha exclaimed and froze the image of a man walking into the frame. 'Colin Deed,' she said. 'It must be him as he's wearing similar clothes to the description his mother gave us.'

Sasha ran the video on.

Jo could see Colin was walking unsteadily along the pebbles. But then he stopped and turned slightly, towards the camera. 'Is there anyone else on the tape?' she asked Sasha. 'Only he seems to be talking to someone.'

'Not that I can find.'

'How peculiar.'

'He seems happy enough,' said Byrd. 'Look he's smiling, waving his arms around and nodding. It's just as though he were having a conversation.'

'He's definitely talking,' said Jo. 'He could just be talking to himself. You know, talking to someone, but it's all in his head.'

'Schizophrenia,' said Jill. 'Hearing voices.'

'Is he on a mobile phone?'

'Can't see one,' said Ken. 'Not even ear buds.'

'No, you're right, there's no sign of a phone,' said Byrd and as he spoke Colin ambled away out of the range of the camera.

'So he was on Pagham beach that night.'

Byrd nodded. 'But it doesn't tell us much else, apart from the fact that he might be mentally ill.'

'Don't you think his parents would have noticed something wrong with him if he were displaying issues with his mental health?' asked Jill. 'Or his work colleagues?'

'I agree,' said Jo, 'they all would. So I doubt that's it.

It's more likely someone who we can't see.'

'A friend? Another resident? Neighbour? Dog walker? A mugger?'

'Something like that,' Jo agreed with Ken. 'Go over the results from the door to door enquiries. See if anyone else was out and about that night. They might have seen someone other than Colin and haven't realised the importance of what they've seen.'

'Right oh, Guv.'

'We need to know who, or what, he was talking to.'

'Or what?' Jill frowned.

'Sorry,' Jo said quickly. 'Slip of the tongue.'

But it was more than a slip of the tongue. For Jo was beginning to realise that they could be up against something far more evil than a random mugger.

CHAPTER 13

Having sent a team of uniformed officers back to Pagham, all Jo could do was wait. But, impatient by nature, she was struggling to find tasks that would eradicate her worry over Colin and his whereabouts. The longer the investigation went on without any results, it could indicate that there was less and less chance of him being found alive.

Then her computer pinged with an email and Jo ran with the distraction. Opening the mail programme she found it was from Sasha. She'd managed to access Colin's laptop and had provided Jo with a link and the password for an on-line group.

Eagerly Jo clicked on the link… and came face to face with a suicide forum. Jo's eyes widened in horror, as she skimmed the contents. There were 'ENDING IT ALL' rooms where you could learn about the best methods to take your own life. 'SUPPORT' thread, which was nothing of the sort, simply let you share the details of your forthcoming suicide and read encouraging conversations to spur you on and get it done. 'GET IT OFF YOUR CHEST' gave members a platform for lambasting parents, siblings and partners who had not been supportive and pushed users to the very edge of their sanity.

Jo couldn't read anymore and closed the lid of her laptop with a thud. She stood, but not knowing where to go, she paced her office like a caged animal. She had no idea such sites existed. How horrendous to think Colin's mind and life were in such a muddle that he had seriously contemplated suicide. This case was turning into a nightmare. Someone, somewhere, could be encouraging people to commit suicide. Had Colin succumbed to that encouragement? Did he really feel his life wasn't worth living after his relationship with Claire failed? Was he dispirited by the empty sex he found from dating sites? He must have thought that whatever he did, or wherever he went, made no difference. He was alone, depressed, yet armed with knowledge about how to kill himself to make the pain go away. But is that what he'd done? Had he not thought about the pain his suicide would cause his parents, wider family, and friends? Could he have been that selfish and self-absorbed?

Jo had to get out. She needed fresh air and space to clear her head. As she walked out of her office she called to Sasha, 'If anyone wants me, I'm on my mobile. Oh and can you do a search for suicides in the area.'

'OK. What is it you're looking for?'

'I need to know if there's a local hot spot for suicides. Either on land or by the sea? You know, like the cliffs in Brighton were popular for a while, until they put up all the fences. That sort of thing.'

'OK, you're the boss.'

Jo ran down the concrete stairs that would take her to the front of the station and out into fresh air. Sasha was right. She was the boss. And the buck would stop with her. She wasn't convinced Colin had committed suicide, but she owed it to him and to his family to find the truth. No matter how farfetched that truth may seem.

CHAPTER 14

Jill stood at the front door of the Deed house. She opened and closed her hands, trying to relax before the task ahead. She was about to meet Mr and Mrs Deed for the first time and to become their point of contact for the investigation. At some point in the future, they may be allocated a dedicated Family Liaison Officer, depending upon the outcome of their current enquiries.

The opening of the door took her by surprise. 'Oh, hello, I'm DC um Sandy.'

'Thought so, lass. Come on in.'

The man was grey haired and slow of movement, but the smile he gave her appeared genuine, despite being watery. He was clearly making an effort for her.

'Thank you, Mr Deed,' she said as she walked into the bungalow. It was as neat and tidy inside as outside and she walked along the thick carpet after him into a spacious living room where his wife was sitting. By contrast to Mr Deed, she looked in bad shape. Her face was pale but with splotches of red, her eyes looked sore and bloodshot and she was wearing mis-matched clothes and slippers.

'Hello, Mrs Deed, I'm DC Sandy.'

Jill didn't get a response and it seemed Mrs Deed had

turned in on herself. Her eyes were blank, and she appeared to be looking at a spot over Jill's shoulder, so much so that Jill turned to see if anyone was behind her. But all she could see was empty space.

Jill moved from the doorway and sat next to Mrs Deed on the settee. She wanted to take the woman's hand but didn't think she should. Not yet. They didn't know each other, and Jill wouldn't invade Mrs Deed's personal space.

'I'm here for support and to try to answer any questions you have. I'll also be the one who will keep you updated on the investigation. Do you understand?'

There was the faintest of nods from Mrs Deed. Her husband walked into the room with a tray of drinks. 'I was just making a brew, so I did one for you. Do you have sugar in your tea?'

'No thanks,' Jill smiled at the kind gesture. 'Okay, so as I was just explaining to your wife, I'll be providing a single point of contact for you. I'll be able to answer your questions and provide regular updates on the case. I've a few leaflets here about support services, including the Missing People charity. You should let me know of any concerns you may have about the investigation. I'll be able to give you realistic updates on what is being done and how the investigation is being conducted.'

Mr Deed nodded and said, 'Thank you, that will be extremely helpful. Won't it, Flo?'

'I should have known.'

'Known what, Mrs Deed?'

'That he was depressed, having a bad time, whatever. I should have encouraged him to speak to me. I always thought he knew he could tell me anything.'

'Now, now, Flo,' Mr Deed soothed. 'You don't know that Colin has committed suicide. I keep telling you that.'

'What else is there? He'd never go away and not tell us. Not Colin. It's all my fault. It must be.'

At that point Jill decided to take Mrs Deed's hands. They were lying in her lap and trembling. 'Please you mustn't blame yourselves. There is a natural tendency to do that, I know, but you must try not to.'

Mrs Deed turned look at Jill. Tears were rolling down her cheeks unchecked. Jill's heart bled for the woman. She'd done some grief counselling through the Cathedral, with a mentor, after she'd obtained her degree in psychology, and it was always a harrowing event for all involved.

She tried to explain further to Mr and Mrs Deed. 'Grief is a natural response to loss. It's the emotional suffering you feel when something or someone you love is taken away. Often, the pain of loss can feel overwhelming. You may experience all kinds of difficult and unexpected emotions, from shock or anger to disbelief, guilt, and profound sadness. The pain of grief can also disrupt your physical health, making it difficult to sleep, eat, or even think straight. These are normal reactions to loss—and the more significant the loss, the more intense your grief will be. But rest assured your reactions are normal. Try to go with them and not fight against them.'

Jill wasn't sure that Mrs Deed had heard her, but Mr Deed seemed to have done, as he was nodding.

'Thanks love, those were kind words. And by the way, please call me Del and that is Flo. Can we call you Jill?'

'Of course you can.'

Jill knew that there were healthy ways to cope with the pain that, in time, can ease sadness and help with coming to terms with loss, find new meaning, and eventually moving on with life. But now was not the time for such advice. Maybe later. When they knew what had happened to Colin.

'What do you think might have happened to him, Del?'

'He might have done something silly. Met someone and something's gone wrong. Gone off with them maybe?

I know he was lonely. He could have been easy pickings for someone.'

'Someone?'

'Yes, group, or cult, or something. Oh, I don't know. I'm just clutching at straws, I guess. Anyway I think I'll see if I can persuade Flo to go to bed and rest for a while. The doctor's been and left her some pills to help her sleep.'

Jill nodded. 'Let's hope they help her.' She stood to leave. 'I'll pop over tomorrow to see how you're both doing. But obviously if there's any news…' she trailed off, not really wanting to go there. Instead she continued, 'I can see myself out. Goodbye, Flo.' Jill looked down at Colin's mother, but got no response.

As Jill walked into the hall, Mr Deed followed her and shut the living room door behind him.

'I wanted a quick word in private,' he said and opened the front door.

They stepped outside and he handed Jill a padded envelope. She took it and realised it felt like there was a small book inside.

'This is a diary I found hidden in Colin's bedroom. I don't want Flo to know about it.'

Jill frowned.

'You'll realise why when you read it.'

'Alright, thanks Mr… Del. And if there's anything you want to know, or anything you need, give me a ring, won't you?'

Del nodded his agreement then went back inside to his wife.

Once Jill got back in the car, she opened the envelope and withdrew a diary. Flicking through it, it seemed that Colin had been keeping a lot from his parents. About his feelings and his activity on FANCY.

The diary was a catalogue of the girls he'd met, what they'd done and even giving them scores! She dreaded to think what his father had made of it. But what mattered now was how the team felt about it. Jill started the car and made her way back to the police station as quickly as she could.

CHAPTER 15

Jo was in her office when Jill got back.

'Got a minute, Boss?'

'Of course, Jill, in you come. How was it with Mr and Mrs Deed?'

Jill explained the sorry state Flo was in and Jo's heart wept for her. Loss was one of the hardest emotional things to live with. The death of a loved one... but Jo had to pull her thoughts away from her own mother's death as Jill was speaking again.

'But that's not all,' she said. 'His dad gave me an envelope. In it is a diary. Colin's diary. Del found it hidden in the house somewhere.'

'And?'

'And you need to read it.' Jo gulped. 'It's mostly about his activities with girls. Those he met online, those he met locally and holidaymakers.'

'Holidaymakers?'

'There's a large holiday camp about a mile from the bungalow.'

'Oh God,' said Jo, 'that's going to give us problems.'

Jill nodded. 'By all accounts the holiday park is huge. One of the biggest in the area.'

'Why didn't we know about this earlier?' Jo demanded.

'We, um, felt it was too far away to be relevant. And Pagham is so quiet, we figured people from there went to the busier places. You know… Bognor, Chichester. It was unlikely the guests there would have anything to do with the Pagham locals.'

Jo's anger evaporated. Jill was right. Uniformed officers had gone all through Pagham as that was in the immediate vicinity of Colin's home. Getting them to go through the holiday park would be like canvassing Bognor, the nearest busy town. Like looking for a needle in a haystack. But still, she should have been aware of it.

'The turnover of visitors will make it hard to trace anyone who came into contact with Colin,' she said. 'Give the camp office a ring and ask if there's any way they can help the investigation. And leave the diary here, I want to have a look through it before I pass it onto the rest of the team.'

Jill nodded and she handed Jo the envelope.

'Good, now off you go and close the door behind you.'

Once Jill had left Jo opened the envelope. She drew out a slim diary. Opening the black cover there was a page with 'Colin's little black book!' written on it.

As Jo opened it, she was immediately jolted against the back of her chair. Her vision narrowed to the book. Everything else faded to black. Then the photographs started. It was like looking at a kaleidoscope. Faces of young girls flashed by. Round and round they went. Some smiling, some laughing, some crying. Crying? On and on the faces went until Jo couldn't take any more and threw the diary on her desk.

The vision faded and Jo was once more in her office. Drained. Upset. And, if she were honest, a little frightened. She glanced down at the page the book had fallen open at and touched it.

She was in a car. She didn't know where, as it was dark outside the windows. She was sat in the front passenger seat and turned to find two people in the car with her on the backseat. Colin was one and the other… it was hard to see her face as it was shielded from Jo by Colin. The girl was distressed. She kept saying, 'No, no, please no.' Colin wasn't taking any notice. He had her pinned down with his body and her hands were held above her head, being pushed against the rear door window. The girl was sobbing, but Colin was laughing. 'Fuck the lot of you,' he said. 'You're all whores, slags, you're going to get what you deserve.'

Jo called out, 'Stop!' and reached out to touch - nothing.

She pushed the hated diary away from her. The visions were too much for Jo to handle. It seemed that Flo and Derek's beloved son was nothing more than a sexual predator. Jo felt sick to her stomach as she lifted her internal phone to call for Byrd.

CHAPTER 16

Jo showed Byrd the diary, then went to get coffees while he read it. Returning, she saw him put it back in the envelope and lay it carefully on Jo's desk.

'Well?' she said from the door.

Byrd blew out a breath. 'Jesus, it seems our Colin reckons himself as a bit of a stud.'

'Yeah, but he comes across as more of a predator, don't you think?'

Byrd narrowed his eyes. 'Is that how it came across to you?' he asked, choosing his words carefully.

Jo knew he was intimating that she'd had a vision. She nodded. 'Very much so.'

'So, where do we go from here?'

'That's the thing,' she said. 'It's all checks and balances, information versus assumption. Information about Colin and his lifestyle should guide the investigation, contribute to assessing the risk to him and help us identify the possible reasons for his absence. All we can do is collate as comprehensive picture as we can, from information from his family, friends, behaviour, hobbies and habits and see where it takes us.'

'Which is where?'

'I'm fucked if I know,' she had to admit ruefully. 'Everything about him is contradictory. The way his parents see him, versus what he is really like. He shows one part of himself to them, another to his cousin, one face to his work colleagues and yet another to girls he meets.' Jo indicated the diary. 'That is an appalling testament to the worst side of Colin's personality. It's cruel, demeaning, and violent. Reading that one could be forgiven for thinking he's holed up with some woman as his plaything. We can't tell his parents that!'

'I agree, but Derek Deed has read it hasn't he?'

'Maybe bits, maybe all of it, we don't know at this stage. But his mother doesn't know of its existence.'

Byrd had a slurp of his coffee then said, 'Our dilemma then is that individuals have the right to privacy and do not have to inform their families and friends about their whereabouts.'

'You're right,' said Jo. 'But suddenly stopping all habitual activity is certainly a cause for concern.'

'So what's the next step?'

'The media.'

CHAPTER 17

Jo looked out at the sea of faces – the dreaded media. They weren't bad overall, but the tiny pockets of reporters determined to write about any sleaze they could find, or make up, about an on-going police investigation, were always a threat. Jo and the team had decided to do a media appeal on the disappearance of Colin Deed, as on balance they needed help and hoped that the British public would respond. Unfortunately, there was always the risk of crank calls that could divert the investigation down rabbit holes. Jo took a deep breath and spoke.

'Thank you all for coming. Thank you...' and she waited as the room settled. 'We're asking for the public's help with any information they can give us regarding the disappearance of Colin Deed. He was last seen five days ago in Pagham, on the coast between Chichester and Bognor. Did anyone meet him or see him on the night of Monday the 7th? Passed him in the street? Saw him in a local pub? We would also like to hear from anyone staying at the nearby holiday park on the edge of the nature reserve, that has been in contact with him, spoken to him, or seen him whilst they were there on holiday. We realise that visitors to our region could live anywhere in the UK and we are therefore grateful to the national media for responding to our request for help. His parents, Derek and Florence Deed are understandably deeply distressed and worried about their son.'

The Deeds were sat next to Jo on the long table set up at the front of the room, but it had been agreed that they wouldn't speak.

'Over the past five days Colin hasn't been at work, nor touched his bank account. His passport is still at home so early indications are that he's not left the country. This behaviour is not normal for Colin, which is why it's rung alarm bells. He's a very conscientious employee and a member of a close-knit family.'

'Is this a murder enquiry?' someone asked. Jo couldn't see who but decided to answer the question anyway. Glancing at Flo she saw the question had triggered a fresh bout of tears, which could well have been what the reporter wanted, as the number of motorized clicks from cameras increased.

'Absolutely not. This is a missing person enquiry.'

'So you're hoping that he's still alive somewhere.'

'Yes we are. Ladies and gentlemen there are full details in your press packs but if you have any more questions, please direct them to the Press Office. At this time Mr and Mrs Deed will not be speaking, nor taking questions. Thank you.'

Jo stood, as did Byrd and Jill Sandy and they ushered Mr and Mrs Deed out of the room. Flo was barely hanging on and Byrd moved to take her arm and hold her up. Del Deed was having problems of his own and so Jill moved to his side. Between them the two officers led the Deeds to chairs that had been sent up in a nearby conference room. Jill then busied getting everyone coffees from the percolator in the corner.

Del pressed a hot drink into his wife's hand then said to Jo, 'Do you think that will have helped? I hate to think we've put Flo through this for nothing.'

Jill was sat at the table next to Mrs Deed and was trying to persuade her to take a few sips of the hot drink. The poor woman had aged 10 years in the past five days. Her hands trembled, her hair seemed to have turned white overnight and the small smear of lipstick she was wearing for the cameras was stuck in clumps to her chapped lips. Already she was the ghost of the woman she'd been before Colin went missing. Jo's face hardened at the thought that Colin could have deliberately gone missing and done this to his poor mother. No one deserved being treated like that.

'I'm sorry,' Mrs Deed whispered. 'But I'd like to go home now.'

They all stood. 'Of course,' Jo said. 'Thank you for coming, I know how difficult this has been for you. There's a car waiting downstairs to take you home.'

Mr Deed stopped and turned back to Jo. 'You'll be in touch…'

Jo nodded. 'Of course. DC Sandy will keep you informed.'

Del Deed nodded and then walked rather unsteadily out of the room. Jo sank back into her chair and put her head in her hands. She felt Byrd slip his arm around her shoulder and pull her towards him. 'It's alright,' he whispered in her hair. 'We'll find him.'

Jo took comfort from Byrd's presence and his words. She nodded. They had to believe that. Anyway, let's face it, things couldn't get much worse, she reasoned.

But then they did.

CHAPTER 18

Driving home that night Jo was exhausted. The hedges rushed by on both sides of the car as she negotiated the country lanes, closing in on her, brushing the paintwork as she passed. Sometimes living outside Chichester was like a balm to her soul, at others a real pain when all she wanted to do was to fall into bed.

The day had been particularly harrowing. Mr and Mrs Deed were barely holding up. So far there hadn't been any sightings of Colin reported by the public. She hoped the whole thing hadn't been a waste of time. As she drove, she chewed her lip with worry. There were too many unknowns in this case. Where did Colin spend his spare time? Who with? They were trying to trace the girls he'd met up with, but so far, the dating site FANCY were proving to be particularly unhelpful, citing data protection, client privacy and protecting their reputation. It was a shame they didn't care as much for Colin as they did their shareholders. Clearly, Jo would have to come up with a body and get a warrant before the dating site would open their database and help the police. Jo could understand their reluctance but was deeply frustrated by it.

Negotiating a bend in the road, Jo dropped down a gear. As she entered the left-hand curve, she saw headlights coming towards her. They were on full beam and Jo started to squint, thinking the driver would flick them down. But it didn't happen. As the car got closer, the lights grew in intensity until they were filling the little Mini. Jo was completely blinded and had slowed, cursing the foolish driver, and raised her arm in an attempt to protect her eyes. If only she could see the car to get at least the make and model, but there was no chance of that.

A flash of lightening lit up the night and Jo had the impression that it wasn't just a car bearing down on her, but a horse, rearing up, prancing on hind legs, and heading straight for Jo. It seemed at once part of the brightness yet solidifying the nearer it got to her car. Looming over her. Malevolent. She screamed as the horse landed on her bonnet, the sickening crunch of metal loud in the stillness of the night.

Jo yanked hard on the steering wheel, pulling the car to the left, heading for the hedge. As she ploughed into it, she was jerked backwards into the seat as her belt ratchet worked and held her. Then with a pop the airbag deployed, and it cradled her face in its white folds. The engine cut out and there was a sudden silence. The night was once more inky black. All trace of the other car gone. No headlights. No horse. Nothing.

Shaking and close to tears Jo pulled the handle on the driver's door, but it was stuck. Leaning her weight against it and banging it with her hands didn't help. It was jammed solid. Not wanting to stay in the car in case of an electrical fire, or igniting petrol, Jo managed to clamber over the central console and into the passenger seat. Thankfully that door opened, and Jo tumbled out onto the grass verge. Taking a moment, she sat on the wet grass, smelling burnt oil and exhaust fumes. Her headlights were still on but were now lighting up the hedge they were buried in, and not the road. Pulling herself up with the aid of the car seat, Jo leaned into the interior and reached for the emergency call button on her car. Her fingers just had enough energy to push it, before she collapsed back onto the grass verge, panting and crying, to await assistance.

CHAPTER 19

Eddie was following Jo home in his car. Driving through the twisting, winding roads, he was enjoying the freedom after a gruelling day at the office. He was also turning over the case in his mind as he drove. And so he wasn't really paying attention as he rounded a tight left-hand bend. Suddenly faced with the rear of Jo's car halfway across the road, he slammed on his brakes and came to a sliding stop. Turning on his emergency lights, he left his car where it was and clambered out, screaming Jo's name. He couldn't understand what might have happened. Jo was a very competent driver and had done the police advanced driving course, so for her to lose control of the car and finish up buried in a hedge didn't compute.

He screamed her name again, and was rewarded with a small voice calling, 'I'm here.'

Spotting her sitting on the grass verge, partly obscured by the rear end of her car, he hurried to her side.

'Dear God, woman, what the hell have you done now?' Fear for her safety was making his voice gruff. As he dropped to crouch next to her and gather her in his arms, he realised that he was shaking as much as she was.

'A c c car,' she stuttered.

'Forced you off the road?'

Jo nodded. 'Lights. Couldn't see. Blinded me.'

'Deliberate, do you think? Or just an accident.'

Jo took a shaky breath. 'Deliberate. Police and a recovery vehicle are on their way.'

Eddie moved to sit down next to Jo, ignoring the damp that was seeping into his trousers. 'That was quick.'

She nodded. 'Mini assist.'

'Right. Look can you walk to my car, or should I call an ambulance for you.'

Jo shook her head and bits of windscreen glass fell out of it, making Byrd smile. 'No ambulance, I'm just a bit shaken up.'

'Come on then, you,' and Byrd stood and reached out his hand to Jo.

He led her to his car and put her in the passenger seat. By the time he'd parked his car safely on the grass verge the first patrol car arrived. Giving Jo the takeaway coffee he'd been drinking before the accident, he went to meet the officers and help set up a diversion. The rumble of the recovery truck split the night air and Eddie went and sat with Jo while the car was pulled out of the hedge.

'Let's go and see,' said Jo.

'No, you're alright, stay there.'

But Jo was already opening the passenger door and climbing out, making Byrd wonder what she was expecting to see. Intrigued he hurried after her.

With a screech of metal and clods of earth flying in every direction, Jo's car was pulled from the hedge. The front was nothing more than a mangled metal mess. All the lights were smashed, the front grill pushed so far back into the engine it could no longer be seen.

The bonnet was concertinaed at the front, but was intact albeit pushed back towards the windscreen, which had smashed and popped out.

Calling to a police officer and then taking his torch, Jo

shone it on the bonnet.

'What are you looking for?' asked Byrd.

'Those.' Jo pointed to dents in the metal.

Byrd ran his hand over the red painted panel. On it were horseshoe shaped indents. He took Jo's arm and pulled her back into his car.

'What the hell are those dents?' he demanded. The night was turning into a right rollercoaster of emotions, but the overriding one in that moment, was of fear.

'They are horse hooves.'

'No shit, Sherlock.'

'Don't be like that.' Jo took a shaky breath. 'When the car was blinding me, I thought I saw the outline of a horse in the dazzling white light. It's all a bit of a blur, but I'm pretty sure that's what it was.'

Byrd ran his hand over his face. 'Alright, I'll bite. Why would a horse have reared up in front of your car? There's no other evidence that there was a horse on the road, or on the grass verge. Are there even any stables in the area? And why would there be a horse loose at night?'

Jo took a sip of the coffee.

'That must be stone cold by now,' he said taking it from her and putting it in the cup holder. 'Stop avoiding the questions.'

'No, there aren't any stables around here, not that I'm aware of anyway.'

'Any horses in nearby fields?'

Jo shook her head. 'I've never seen any.'

'So how do we explain the dents?'

The longer Jo stayed quiet, the more concerned Byrd became. She obviously had something to tell him. But when would she do that? What the hell was going on?

'It must have been something else, not a horse. Perhaps it was just a trick of the main beam lights of the car, or something,' she finished lamely.

Byrd didn't believe a word of it, but guessed he'd just

have to wait until Jo was ready to tell him. But his sense of unease persisted as he drove them both to Jo's flat.

CHAPTER 20

Jo and Byrd were woken by the buzzing of Jo's doorbell. She opened one eye. It was barely light. What the hell? She wished whoever it was would just go away and maybe they would if she ignored the noise. But as she snuggled into Byrd her eyes snapped open. She was in the middle of a missing person enquiry. Something must have happened.

'Byrd,' she shouted as she leapt out of bed and ran to the intercom. Not bothering to speak she simply released the door lock and waited, pulling on sweats that had been left on the sofa last night.

There were heavy footsteps on the stairs and Jo called for Byrd again. Just as he walked from the bedroom Jo's father burst into the living room. In his arms were daily newspapers. A lot of them.

'Dad, what the hell's wrong? I thought we had a dead body.'

'We will have soon,' he growled and spread half a dozen papers out on the kitchen table. 'Yours.'

Every one of the newspapers carried lurid headlines.
Lothario.
Twisted rapist.

Sexual Predator.
Dangerous and Deranged.
Wanted!

'What the hell?' said Jo. Then the penny dropped. 'The diary.'

'But we told the Press Office we needed to keep the diary and the sexual predator bit quiet from the press!' said Byrd.

'Then it looks like someone forgot that salient bit of information,' said Mick to Byrd. 'I'd taken Honey for a walk into the village, when I saw the papers lined up outside the newsagents. Couldn't believe my bloody eyes, I can tell you.'

'So you stole them!' Jo burst out.

'Of course not. What do you take me for? I pushed a tenner into their letter box. Then Honey and I raced back home. I figured you needed a heads up on this lot.'

Jo turned to Byrd. 'Del and Flo!' Her eyes widened in horror at the thought of what this might do to Mrs Deed, who wasn't in the best of health.

'I'll ring Jill,' said Byrd and ran back into the bedroom.

Honey clattered up the stairs and into the room, looking very pleased with herself. Her tail was wagging, she was panting and dripping water from her open mouth. Jo managed a fleeting smile. She wasn't really a dog person, but her present to her dad on his birthday had been one of her better ideas. Concerned that Mick, a retired police detective, wasn't taking enough care of himself and hardly ever exercising, she decided a dog would give him a companion, an interest, and a reason for taking walks. He now went out on the South Downs every day with his Labrador and they were rarely apart. And it seemed Honey had every reason to be pleased with herself that morning. If she hadn't needed walking, Mick wouldn't have found the papers.

Jo dropped to her knees. 'Good girl, Honey,' she said, rubbing the dog's head and ears. Then she straightened. 'I'd better go, Dad.'

He nodded, called for his dog and together they left Jo's flat above the garage. Jo watched through the window as they ambled back into the main house. Then her gaze once more fell on the newspapers. She leafed through them. It couldn't really be any worse. Every paper mentioned Colin's sordid past. One even had an interview with Claire, his ex-girlfriend. How they'd found her God only knew and Jo wondered how much money the girl had been paid for her kiss and tell story.

Byrd came back, mobile in hand. 'Jill's getting dressed now and going straight to Mr and Mrs Deed. Is it bad?' he nodded at the papers.

'Worse than bad,' Jo replied as her own mobile rang. Grabbing it she looked at the caller display. Mr Deed. 'Bloody fucking awful,' she said to Byrd.

CHAPTER 21

Del Deed had been up early. In truth he hadn't really been asleep, only dozed on and off all night. By 6am he couldn't bear to be in bed any longer and got up, sliding out of bed for fear of waking Flo. Mind you, she'd been pretty much out of it all night after taking a sleeping tablet.

Whilst making a cup of tea he turned on the small television in the kitchen. And saw something he'd never thought he'd see. His son's face up close and personal on breakfast television. But they didn't seem to be treating his disappearance with any sort of respect. And then one of the presenters held up a newspaper. "Dirty and Dangerous!" read the headline. The pretty girl presenter with over-white teeth was saying that there was a nationwide manhunt for a desperate rapist. And that man was Colin.

Del dropped his cup, which shattered on the floor. Then he turned and ran out of the house, intent on going to the local paper shop. By the time he returned with a copy of each national paper, Flo was standing in the middle of the kitchen. There was blood on the floor where she'd trodden on the broken crockery and cut her feet, but she wasn't taking any notice of it. The only thing she could seem to see was the television, which was yet again showing a picture of Colin. She turned to look at Del then slowly spiralled all the way down to the floor. She didn't even try to break her fall and so banged her head against the leg of the table as she fell. Dumping the papers and running to her side, he gathered her into his arms, then, with some difficulty, carried her back to bed. He cleaned the blood from her feet and the gash on her head, but she didn't respond. Occasionally she opened her eyes, but they were blank. Empty. Flo had gone. Del could only hope it wasn't for good.

Hearing a noise downstairs, he patted Flo's hand, then left her to rest. Walking into the kitchen he saw DC Jill Sandy sweeping up the broken pieces of the cup.

'Leave them alone,' he said.

Jill straightened and started to speak. 'Mr Deed I'm…'

But he interrupted her. 'Leave. My. House.' He didn't shout. He was way past that.

'Please let me help…'

'Don't you think you've done enough damage? You've not found Colin. All you've achieved is to turn the whole of England against him! I told you I wanted to keep that diary a secret from Flo, and now everyone knows about it! How could you? How could you?' He shook his head. 'I've already told that boss of yours that we want to be left alone. Now go away.'

Finally the dam broke, and tears began to roll down his cheeks. He fell into a chair and putting his head in his hands sobbed for his wife, for his son and for the life they'd lost.

CHAPTER 22

Jo was driving into work when her mobile rang. Her mini had been towed to the Mini dealer in Chichester, so she'd borrowed her dad's car. Looking at the Bluetooth display she saw it was from Sykes. Should she answer while driving? She thought not. It was going to be a hell of a conversation and she'd be better served by concentrating on the road. But on the other hand, it could make him even angrier than he, no doubt, already was. Taking a deep breath she took the call.

'Jo. 8am. My office.'

The call ended. He'd cut her off. She looked at the time on her dashboard. 7.45am. It was a good job she was nearly at the station.

Fifteen minutes later she was stood outside Sykes' door. Through the glass panel she could see him with the Detective Chief Superintendent, who turned, saw Jo, and opened the door.

'Jo,' he nodded as he walked past her.

'Sir,' she managed, expecting him to start to berate her. But he said nothing and continued on his way. Frowning, she entered Sykes' office.

Copies of newspapers were strewn across his desk. 'I

take it this is your handiwork?' he spat.

'Not exactly, Sir, no.' Jo hated dropping anyone in it, but this was a mistake with far reaching repercussions. Career changing ones. And as much as she was supportive of junior officers, this time she had to think of herself and her team.

'Pray do tell.'

'We've been liaising with the press office and laid out all the relevant facts of the case, so that they could easily answer any questions and deflect the ones that touched on information we weren't commenting on.'

'That was,' Sykes looked down at a notebook, 'DC Moore.'

She nodded. 'That's correct, Sir. It seems that DC Moore let slip more information than we wanted to share. Namely a diary that Colin Deed had been keeping about his sexual encounters. Once one of the papers had wind of it, the news went viral, hence all the lurid headlines.'

'And the pieces on national breakfast television.'

'Yes, Sir.'

'So once again it's not the great Jo Wolfe's fault. Is that what you're telling me?'

Jo didn't answer.

Sykes stood and jabbed a finger at her. 'Have you ever thought it was your fault for telling the boy in the first place? Or is your ego so big that you think you can do what you want and damn the consequences?'

Jo bristled. She wasn't going to be intimidated, at least not by Sykes. 'That's a bit unfair, Sir, I didn't know how inexperienced he was.'

'Unfair comes with the territory, Jo. Get used to it. You'd better not make any more mistakes like this. If you do… well I won't have any choice but to replace you. For the moment it seems you've got the ear of senior officers in this station. But let me tell you that won't last forever. I'll have the last laugh when you make one mistake too many. I'll have you drummed out of Chichester police station quicker than you can say Mick Wolfe. Now get out of my sight.'

Jo nodded, then turned and fled. It looked like her dad had saved her skin by being a friend of the Detective Chief Supt, and pleading her case directly to him, bypassing Sykes. But Sykes was clearly out to get her. As she walked down the concrete steps to the next floor, she wondered why her boss was so jealous? Because that's how it seemed. He was jealous of Jo and her career and her good reputation within Chichester. Or was it her dad he hated? Anger and jealousy were two potent emotions and the thought that Sykes could seriously derail her career sent a shiver down Jo's back.

CHAPTER 23

Combing through past cases to try and find any similar ones to Colin's disappearance, one in particular made Jill stop and look more closely. It concerned a young man, Alex, who disappeared about six months before Colin, and was last seen in the Chichester Marina area just around the coast from Pagham. The similarities were young man, Pagham and missing presumed dead. In all other respects the two men varied greatly.

Colin came from a middle-class background; Alex from a poor one.

Colin had a good job; Alex didn't have one.

Colin had no debts; Alex had many of them including rent arrears.

Colin didn't do drugs; Alex did.

Colin had good mental health (at least he did before the breakdown of his relationship); Alex was bi-polar.

Colin would not have disappeared; Alex almost certainly would.

There were a great many disparities between the two cases, but Jill picked up the phone to get a better sense of Alex. In the file was a statement from a friend, Stephen Sumner, who had known Alex since their school days.

She called his mobile and was rewarded with an answer.

After introducing herself, she asked if he had a few minutes to talk about Alex.

'Is there something new? Have you found him?'

'I'm afraid not,' Jill had to confess. 'But I've been going through the file and wondered if you could answer a couple of questions for me. We're having another look at Alex's disappearance as part of a regular review.'

'Oh, oh, I see. For a moment there, I thought... well, anyway... what can I help you with?'

'I understand Alex had some, shall we say, difficulties in life.'

'If you mean he wasn't clean living, did drugs, hadn't worked for a while, was behind in his rent, then yeah life wasn't too good for poor Alex. I did what I could to help, but I've very little money myself.'

'I'm sure you did,' soothed Jill. 'What was his mental health like?'

'You mean his diagnosis of bi-polar?'

'Yes. How did that affect him?'

'Well he didn't manage it properly.'

'No? Did he take any medication?'

'No. There was a lot of denial going on. If I take them, I'm admitting I'm bipolar kind of thing. To be honest I always thought he liked the highs. He didn't like the way the tablets flattened everything out. Mind you it wasn't good when he had the really bad bouts of depression.'

'I understand he'd attempted suicide in the past?'

'Well, yeah, but that was years ago, both times after he'd had a bad trip, you know. He hadn't done anything like that for years.'

'But he could have been depressed when he disappeared?'

'I guess.'

'And could have committed suicide?'

'I suppose so, but I'll never believe it. He loved life

too much. Something's happened to him. It's just that I don't know what. Please don't give up on him!'

Jill didn't really know how to respond to that, so she said, 'Thanks for your time, and for your candour. We'll be in touch if there are any developments.' That was the best she could come up with.

As Jill replaced the receiver she pondered. Two young men. Both went missing in the same area. Both families and friends insisted they wouldn't have committed suicide. But if that were the case, then where the hell where they?

And where there any more cases?

It was time to speak to Jo.

CHAPTER 24

Jo listened as Jill recounted her review of the case of Alex Simms and her telephone conversation with his friend.

'Hmm,' pondered Jo. 'I wonder if there are any more cases of suspected suicides?'

'Are we saying that it's a possibility that Colin committed suicide?'

'Maybe, maybe not, but we need to look at any and every pattern we can find.'

Jo walked to the door of her office. 'Sasha,' she called, 'can you identify any cases of unsolved missing persons in the area for past two, no, three years? Let's see what you can find.'

'I've no confirmed suicides, but quite a few missing persons, Guv.'

'Oh, you've already done it.'

'It's my job.'

'Yes, yes, of course it is,' said Jo hurriedly, not wanting to inadvertently upset Sasha. 'Well done. So, how many?

'10 over the last few years. Similar cases as far as I can see from the scant details on the computer search.'

'Right, get everything you can on them and pass the

files to Jill and Ken.' She turned to Jill, who had followed her to Sasha's desk. 'You and Ken can contact the families or friends of the missing and ask any questions you may have. Just let them know we're doing our normal review of cold cases.'

'Dear God, can't they find any of them? Or anything of them? No bodies washed up?' said Jill, horrified.

'No, um, that's the whole point, that's why the cases are still open.' Sasha stating the obvious again.

Seeing the look on Jill's face, Jo stepped in and said, 'What about their phones or wallets? If they were washed up on the beach then someone finding them might have presumed they had been lost and either thrown them away, kept them, or handed them in. Sasha, can you try and find correlations with anything taken to any police station as being found, maybe washed up on the beach and handed in to the local police. We may find some items not previously thought to relate to any of these cases.'

Sasha didn't reply, clearly not thinking one was needed. Jo smiled at Jill, then said, 'Byrd you're with me.'

Once they were sat in the car Byrd asked, 'Where are we off to?'

'To see Mr and Mrs Deed. They need to know that we are categorising Colin as missing and as either a suicide or murder victim.'

'In other words missing, presumed dead.'

Jo nodded. 'The thornier issue is 10 men missing over three years, more than two a year. Let's hope Jill and Ken come up with something.'

Byrd didn't look hopeful, then he turned and began driving. On the short drive Jo realised it was about time to tell Byrd and the others of her encounter with a Kelpie. It was looking more and more like it might have a great deal to do with this case. But she wanted to pick her moment.

CHAPTER 25

Mr Deed opened the door in response to their knock. No longer having to identify herself and Byrd, Jo asked if they could have a word. Nodding, he let them into the house and led the way to the sitting room. Mrs Deed didn't look much better than when Jo had last seen her. Clenched hands, silvery white hair, sallow skin, was the overriding impression. Jo felt for the poor woman and wished she had better news.

After sitting down, she haltingly began to tell them that it was looking more and more likely that Colin might have committed suicide.

'Suicide?' Mr Deed looked stricken.

Jo nodded. 'I'm sorry, but yes. There is more evidence to support suicide, than that he's gone off somewhere.' She briefly thought about the suicide forums but decided to keep that piece of information to herself for now. 'It's hard to disappear with no phone and no bank activity.' Jo took a deep breath. She was still in two minds about how much information to share. But the Deed's deserved to know what might be coming down the line. It would hit them like a truck, and she didn't want them blindsided again. Pushing away the vehicle analogies she said, 'This is going to be difficult to hear, but we believe there are examples of other persons going missing in this area. All young men.'

Mrs Deed looked at Jo, wide eyed. 'How many?

Jo paused and swallowed, not sure she could continue with the conversation.

'10 going back several years,' Byrd said.

Jo threw him a look of thanks, as she was becoming overwhelmed with the Deed's pain. Needing to harden her emotions she listened as Byrd said, 'Out of respect for your family we wanted to let you both know before we tell the press that Colin's disappearance could be a missing person enquiry with possible suicide. And that there are others.'

'You've not found any evidence of Colin dead or alive?'

Byrd shook his head. 'No, I'm sorry, a comprehensive search of the area has revealed nothing.'

'So you think he drowned?' Mrs Deed said, gripping the arms of her chair.

'I'm afraid so,' said Jo gently.

'But you haven't found him!' her voice was rising. 'Why haven't you found him?' She stood. 'Have you even tried? I insist you send boats and divers out to try and find his body. Someone must be able to find him!' She fell back into her seat, sobbing, and her husband went over to her.

'Now, now, Flo,' he soothed, stroking her arm.

'I'm sorry but that won't work, we've looked into it. What with tides and the depth of water off Pagham, he'd be more than likely carried out of this natural harbour, into open sea. It's difficult to locate the bodies of drowning victims.'

At that Flo ran from the room. Mr Deed made to follow her and said, 'I'll just see to her.'

'We'll leave you in peace,' Jo said, standing.

'No, hang on a minute, will you? I'll come back down.'

Once he was out of the room, Byrd closed the door and huffed out a breath. 'Not one of my better house calls.'

'I know, its bloody awful this side of the job.'

Jo looked around the room and her gaze fell on a glass statue. She walked over to it, saw it was a design award for Colin. It was a figure etched in glass and she picked it up to have a closer look.

Jo felt a wave crash over her head and spluttered and fought for breath. Then her hand was taken, and she was pulled under and led through the sea by a woman. Slim, dark haired, seemingly wearing a swimsuit. Jo felt Colin's… excitement? Really? He was focused on the young woman, happily following her. Jo wondered if she were some sort of siren, there to lure young men to their deaths.

They approached the mouth of a cave. There appeared to be light coming from inside it and the young woman turned and said to Colin, 'Come on, come in and join me.'

For the first time Jo felt Colin panic. He was struggling and trying to get away, but the woman held on. He couldn't shake her off him. He looked up. There was very little light anymore from the surface. They were too far under the sea. He was out of his depth in more ways than one.

'Come on,' she insisted. 'You know you want to. We can be together forever down here.'

Jo felt Colin relax, resigned to his fate as he allowed himself to be pulled into the cave and disappeared from view.

Then it was Jo's turn to panic. She needed to breathe. Her chest was getting tight with lack of oxygen and the natural reflex to inhale was taking over and winning. Her vision dimmed. She could see white blobs floating on her closed eyelids. Her lungs were burning. She twisted this way and that, but there was no way up, just an endless amount of water. She felt the pressure of it, the blackness of it and... took a breath.

She came out of the vision, doubled over, trying to get air into her lungs. She felt winded. She couldn't breathe. Began hyperventilating. Byrd was with her in seconds. 'Jo, come on, breathe in out, in out. Breathe with me, that's it, in two three, out two three. There you go. Relax. Come on. It's alright, I've got you.'

Slowly Jo's breathing returned to normal and she staggered drunkenly to a chair.

'What the hell was that?' asked Byrd, worry etched in his face and around his eyes and he grabbed her hands.

'I know where Colin is,' she said. 'But you're not going to like it.'

They heard Mr Deed coming back down the stairs.

'First,' she continued, 'we've got to tell Mr Deed about Colin's involvement with suicide forums. And also make it clear that if it's not suicide, the alternative is that Colin's been murdered. It's only fair that he hears all this from us. Shall we toss for it?'

CHAPTER 26

Ken and Jill decided to look at two of the old missing persons cases. One man, Henry, was last seen at Chichester marina, missing presumed drowned. The second, Alex, was out with mates in Chichester and was last seen walking home alone. He'd lived on a houseboat along the canal. He had never been seen since. Again he was missing presumed drowned.

'Let's go and look at the scenes,' suggested Ken. 'They're near each other. It might give us a sense of what we're up against.'

Jill nodded and picked up her bag.

As they drove, she remembered the last time she'd been in that area of Chichester, when they'd been looking for a child who had been taken by an evil entity, the Watcher. She shuddered as she remembered the plan they'd hatched for getting the child back. And then there was the final showdown in the cathedral gardens. But Ken knew nothing of that.

'I wonder what happened to that young girl and her son,' Ken said. 'You know, the one from our last big case.'

'Funny, I was just thinking the same,' Jill said. 'The

council were helping to find her somewhere to live, I understand. So she must still be in the Chichester area.'

'Ah, well, good luck to her. It's never easy bringing up a child on your own.'

'Have you got kids, Ken?'

'Yeah, two, a boy and a girl, but they're all grown up now and have moved away to London. Can't stand the place myself. Too crowded, too fast, you've not got time to take a breath, you know?'

Jill nodded. 'I'm happy to stay around here,' she said, thinking of Osian. If they did make a life together, she wondered where it would be. He was bound to get moved on at some point, even though he wouldn't want to. She knew how much he loved serving the faithful in the cathedral.

Ken drove into the marina and parked in an owner's space. As they climbed out, Jill was struck by how beautiful the marina was. With over 1,000 berths and associated facilities, the yachts and boats stretched away into the distance. The sky was clear and blue, reflecting down to kiss the sea. There was the faint chink that came from ropes on masts as the boats bobbed and weaved on the slowly undulating waves.

'Beautiful isn't it,' said Ken appearing at her side.

'Yes, you wouldn't think that something as awful as death could be harbouring here.'

'Maybe it was a peaceful death, you know, Henry just slipped into the water and slowly sank.'

'No one heard any cries, or disturbance that night. Although to be honest there weren't many boats occupied. But why? Why would Henry do it? Want to take his own life? No one seems to know,' said Jill.

'Who knows what is really in someone's mind, though. Behind the painted face and all that.'

'You mean tears of a clown?'

'Yeah. It seems to be a good catch-all doesn't it,

missing presumed drowned,' said Ken.

'Easy answers to explain the deaths. Must have been an accident. Must have been depressed. Must have been intoxicated.'

'Exactly,' agreed Ken.

'Let's keep digging deeper, checking out the other cases first, before we jump to conclusions. We need to see if we can find the reason behind all the young men that have been missing presumed drowned. There must be a connection. There are too many of them for there not to be.'

Suddenly the beautiful scene of the boatyard that stretched out before Jill, went dark. Looking up, she saw a black cloud had appeared and was obscuring the sun, injecting an air of menace into her day that made her scalp tingle and her brow furrow.

CHAPTER 27

As they now had 10 cases going back three years, of young men missing presumed drowned, Jo told Byrd that she'd better take their findings to Sykes.

'Good luck with that one,' he said grimacing. 'This is one time that I'm glad you're the boss and not me!'

'Thanks, Byrd, just what I needed to make me feel better. You sure know how to treat a girl,' she grinned and walked off.

With every step her good humour faded. She never knew what mood Sykes would be in. It was usually grim when it came to Jo. Other officers had told her that he was fine with them, so it seemed to be only Jo that he'd taken an instant dislike to. She was still wondering what had happened between her father and Sykes to make him have such a jaundiced view of Mick and now Mick's daughter. But her father had just said it wasn't relevant and that Jo must be imagining things. Yet, on the other hand, Mick had stepped in to protect her, so he did have a good idea of how miserable her working relationship with her boss was.

But all that background shit was just that. Shit. Jo just had to keep on shovelling.

She had a list of the cases for Sykes. When she arrived at his office he was on the telephone, so she stood just outside the open door and fiddled with the papers in her hands until he'd finished.

He looked up, 'Oh it's you,' he said.

'Yes, Guv. Got a minute?'

'I suppose, come in,' his voice dripped resignation. As though she were the last person he wanted to see. Ever. But couldn't manage to get rid of.

'We've been working the Colin Deed case, as you know,' she began. 'But it appears that his disappearance isn't an isolated incident.'

'Oh, he's been dead before has he?'

Jo closed her eyes briefly to try and anchor herself. What was the saying? Sarcasm is the lowest form of wit. To be honest Sykes was the lowest form of man, someone whose morals were in the gutter and who thought nothing of abusing those he had power over. 'I mean that there have been others.'

'Other what?'

Jo decided Sykes was being deliberately obtuse and a fork of hatred ran through her from head to toe. 'Other cases of missing young men. 10 in the last three years to be precise,' and she handed him the list. 'All in and around the Chichester area.'

He scanned the page and then laughed.

'Sir?'

'No, no, Jo that isn't the thing at all. There's nothing here to suggest a pattern as far as I can see.'

'But, Guv?'

'No buts, Jo, now work the Deed case and leave it at that. Understood?'

'Understood, Guv.'

'Excellent, now fuck off.'

Jo was stunned. This was the worst Sykes had ever been. Backlash from the Chief Superintendent's interference, Jo guessed. She turned on her heel and stalked out of his office with as much dignity as she could muster. Jo vowed to keep digging. She wasn't giving up. There was clearly a connection. 10 cases over three years wasn't statistically normal. Not for their area. Sasha had crunched the numbers. Jo was going to tell Sykes all that, but he'd not given her a chance to. On the balance of probability there was a serial killer out there. 10 murder victims, not 10 suicides. If she stopped investigating, she'd be playing right into Sykes' hands. She wouldn't give him the satisfaction.

And what's more, Sykes didn't know about the Kelpie. But Jo did.

CHAPTER 28

GRIEVING MOTHER TELLS OF HER HEARTACHE
An exclusive report from our crime correspondent.

Gretta Fernholt, a 60-year-old mother from Chichester, is living a parent's worst nightmare. Her son has been missing for 24 months today and on this bleakest of anniversaries she calls on the public and the police to help her find her boy.

'It was just an ordinary day,' she recalls. 'Jacob had gone to work as normal. When he didn't come home later that day, I just assumed he was either working late or had gone for a drink with friends. By 10pm I was beginning to get worried. I'd had no word from him, which was very unusual. He always let me know where he was. He was a good boy like that. By midnight I was convinced there was something wrong, but it wasn't until 8am the following morning that I rang the police and reported him missing. He should have been at work again by 7 am that morning and hadn't turned up.'

Jacob's empty bedroom is testament to a mother's

love. Nothing has been moved or changed since his disappearance. It's stuck in time, waiting for his return. As is Gretta.

'I can't move on, move forward, get on with my life. There's just this awful limbo. But I won't give up on Jacob. I can't.'

When asked what the police were doing, she was scathing in her criticism. 'Nothing. They've done bugger all. They made a perfunctory search for him and now just say he's missing, presumed dead. It sounds like he was in a war zone, in the military or something,' she spat. 'He's just an ordinary boy living an ordinary life, who one day just didn't come home. I'm convinced something awful has happened to him. He could be lying somewhere, unfound, forgotten and alone.'

What can Mrs Fernholt do now?

'I'm calling on the police and the wider public, not to give up on Jacob. He's out there somewhere. If he's dead, is it too much to ask for someone to find his body? Can't someone help a grieving mother? What if it was you? Your child? Ask yourself, what would you do?'

By digging through the archives, this newspaper has realised that there are now 10 young men who have gone missing over several years in our area. 'This isn't good enough,' said a tearful Mrs Fernholt. 'Not one of them has been found. How many more has there to be before the police do something?'

How many more, indeed?

10 missing young men. 10 grieving families. 10 too many.

When this paper rang the police for a comment, we were told that there was no one available to discuss it. That isn't good enough. So we're calling on the people of Chichester, if you have any information that could help the police, please call them at Chichester police station on 01243 666010.

CHAPTER 29

As Jo left her office, the team were frantically trying to field all the calls coming into Major Crimes from the article in the local newspaper. They were in danger of being overwhelmed and Jo needed to ask Sykes for more bodies. Then realised that was completely the wrong phrase.

What was the matter with her? But she knew really. Whichever way she turned there were problems.

Problems with the investigation – they weren't getting anywhere.

Problems with Sykes – he was clearly out to get her and her team.

Problems with the press – they were only hindering, not helping as they were purporting to do.

Problems with her – she thought she was being stalked by someone/something? An entity embroiled in this case. Perhaps a Kelpie?

She still hadn't told Byrd and the others of her fears. She was picking her moment. And so far, one hadn't arrived.

As she walked towards Sykes' office, Jo could hear him shouting. Her spirits sunk even further. Yes, she'd been expecting anger, but had been hoping it wouldn't be too bad. By the sounds of his raised voice, it was. One of the admin staff fled Sykes' office looking pale.

As Jo stood in the doorway, Sykes caught sight of her and shouted, 'What the bloody hell do you call this?' and he threw the newspaper at her.

Leaving it where it landed, Jo walked up to Sykes' desk. She began to defend her team, but he interrupted.

'Oh no you don't, I want action, not excuses. I told you that you were on shaky ground last time, didn't I? One more leak and you were finished!' he ended with a flourish.

Jo was sure he would have thrown something at her if he could. His malevolent eyes shone with indignation, and was that triumph?

'So come on, who told the press? Was it one of your team? It better not have been if you want to keep your job.'

She tried to explain. 'It was the newspaper themselves, Guv, trolling through their archives. There was no leak,' she said emphatically.

Sykes glowered at her, but as he had no evidence of a leak, he changed tack. 'You'd better go and see this poor mother, Mrs Fernholt.'

'I was going to ring her.'

Sykes exploded again. 'Ring! You're not ducking out of this one, Jo. Go and see her. She deserves to be talked to by a senior detective. That is what you are, isn't it? A senior detective? So go and detect,' he snorted.

Jo couldn't be bothered arguing with him anymore, so she turned on her heel and left. If she'd have said she was going to visit Mrs Fernholt he would have told her to ring the woman and to stop wasting time. She knew she couldn't win with him.

Jo really despised the man. He was given to petty grievances. He was nothing but a bully. He never helped, just criticised. A man who felt the best way to lead was through fear.

But Jo wasn't that easily frightened. There were other things in hell and on earth that she truly feared. And that wasn't a pompous, jealous old man, hurtling towards the end of his career.

CHAPTER 30

Eddie turned off the car engine. 'So, this is going to be another one of those bloody awful conversations I don't want to have,' he said.

Jo and Eddie were sat outside the home of Gretta Fernholt. Jo looked along the street. Estate agents say that you should buy the worst house in the best street, but the Fernholt family home was the worst house in the worst street. She knew there were officers who didn't want to patrol this area and Jo couldn't blame them. It was rife with petty thieves, drug dealers, addicts, unemployed and unkempt adults. But that shouldn't influence them, Jo knew. They were here to see a grieving mother and to apologise for the lack of progress on her son's missing person enquiry.

'Oh well,' said Jo. 'Here goes.'

They climbed out of the car and Eddie locked it. Jo wondered if it would still be in one piece when they returned. She turned and went to knock on the front door, but Mrs Fernholt beat her to it and the door was flung open before Jo could touch it.

'I was wondering when you lot would bother to come and see me,' she said and turned and stalked away. Jo and

Eddie looked at each other in desperation, then followed her to the back of the house. Gretta Fernholt was sat at a tatty kitchen table in a tatty kitchen. On every available surface was stacked dirty crockery and flies buzzed around a bin whose gaping mouth spat out take away cartons, some empty and some full.

'We're sorry for your loss,' said Jo.

'What? What? How dare you! Who said he was bloody dead?' Mrs Fernholt sprang to her feet, knocking over her chair in the process. 'Have you found his body?' she jabbed a finger in Jo's face. 'Have you?' she snarled.

To Jo's relief, Eddie moved to stand between the two women. 'Please, Mrs Fernholt, calm down.'

'Fucking rossers, telling me to calm down,' she grumbled, but picked up her chair and sat on it again.

'You alright, mum?' said a voice from the kitchen door. Jo turned to see a child of about 11 or 12, stood there in a vest top and jogging bottoms that looked like cheap designer rip offs.

'Yes, fine, now piss off.' Mrs Fernholt looked back at Eddie. 'My other son. At least I've got one left I suppose.'

Jo wasn't at all sure what that meant. Taking a deep breath she said, 'We're here to apologise on behalf of Chichester Police.' They weren't, but Jo was desperately trying to put out the fire of Gretta Fernholt's anger. It didn't work.

'Oh, sorry, are you? Well sorry doesn't cut it. It's not your son, your brother, your father is it you stupid cow?' she punched the air with her finger.

The finger thing was clearly one of Greta's traits, used to intimate those she was arguing with. But it didn't wash with Jo.

'I told you lot to listen to me from the start and you wouldn't. This is on you not me,' Greta continued.

'I wasn't at Chichester station at the time,' tried Jo, 'so I can't really comment on the investigation.'

'I don't give a fuck,' Gretta spat. 'You're here now and it is your responsibility. Fancy having to find out from the bloody newspaper reporter that my son was just one of many that are missing. How would you like that if it was your child?' and she stormed out of the room.

Jo was hoping that was the end of it, but no such luck. It seemed Gretta had just gone for a cigarette as she immediately returned to the kitchen.

'So what are you doing about it?' she challenged them.

'Everything possible,' Byrd said.

'Which means?'

'Starting again and going through each disappearance with fresh eyes.'

Gretta Fernholt laughed. 'Fresh eyes, well let me tell you my eyes haven't been so bloody fresh lately.'

Jo had to agree as the woman's eyes were ringed in red by lids that looked sore and swollen.

'Well, if you don't get it right this time with your bloody fresh eyes, I'll be onto the papers again. Although next time I'll talk to the nationals. Sell my story, like. How much do you reckon I'd get for the loss of a son, eh? A thousand quid? Ten thousand? How much is his life worth? Well let me tell you, there's no figure big enough. He was torn away from his family. We miss him every day. We just want him back. Now fuck off and do your job and let me know how you and your bloody fresh eyes get on.'

Jo fled, with Byrd at her heels. She flung open the front door and staggered out into the street. Once in the car she said, 'Sweet Jesus. That was bad.'

Eddie looked stricken and seemed incapable of speech as he nodded his head.

Jo was shaking. She felt suitably chastised. More than that. Flayed. The encounter had left Jo emotionally exposed and vulnerable. Mrs Fernholt may not come from the best of backgrounds, but she was still a mother. Jo felt empathy for the poor woman, but she had to be a calm level-headed detective inspector. Most of the missing were before her time at Chichester, but Mrs Fernholt was right, the families didn't want excuses, they wanted action.

'Come on, Eddie,' she said. 'Let's get back to it. There's nothing more to be accomplished here.'

CHAPTER 31

'DI Jo Wolfe?' said a voice from Jo's door.

She glanced up. 'Yes?'

'Liam Statham, your new press liaison officer.'

Jo looked at the man properly this time. Late thirties, maybe. Suit and tie. Clean and smart. Thank goodness. At least he didn't look like a spotty teenager, like the last one. Hopefully, this one had more experience.

'Hi, Liam, come in and take a seat.'

He walked the couple of steps to a chair by Jo's desk, sat and opened a notebook. 'I'm sorry, Ma'am, but I really need a quote about these young men that are missing. Or would you give a press interview? That would be even better.'

Jo laughed, but without mirth. 'Better for who? Certainly not me.' She thought for a moment. 'I realise that you have to give them something.' The press officer looked relieved. 'The best I can do is a holding message. One encouraging calm, and I suppose we'll have to give them a phone number in case anyone has any evidence or information that could help us. Ask members of the public and press to remain calm and give us the space we need to do our jobs. Is that alright?'

'Not really, Ma'am, no.'

Jo grinned. 'I know that, Liam, but it's the best you're going to get.'

'I can get the calls directed here?'

She nodded. 'Let's use the tip line. That's already set up and let's face it, is never used. The good people of Chichester either don't think we have any crime, or if they know of any are keeping tight lipped about it.'

'Thank you, Ma'am, that will help I'm sure. I'll send something out immediately, so it will hit tonight's papers and local tv news.'

'Thanks, Liam. Are you going to be a permanent fixture at the press office?'

'It seems so, Ma'am.'

'Well good luck with your posting.'

'Thank you,' he said and stood.

'One more thing before you go?'

'Yes?' he stood poised with his notebook once again.

'If we're going to be working together, for God's sake stop calling me Ma'am! Makes me feel about 90.'

Liam grinned, 'Got it.'

As Liam left, Jo ran her hands through her short messy black hair. Although to be fair it was getting straggly and very much in need of a cut. Not that she knew when she'd be able to fit that in. She took a moment to feel sorry for herself. Then stopped. What was wrong with her? Things couldn't get any worse, so the only way was up. She grinned as the chorus of the well-known song filled her head.

The telephone on her desk rang. As the caller started talking, he pieced her bubble of optimism. If she'd thought things couldn't get any worse, she was wrong.

The call was from a London solicitor.

Jo listened without speaking, then put the phone down. She called Byrd in.

'You alright, Boss?' he said from the door.

'Not so you'd notice, no,' said Jo. 'Come in.'

He sat where Liam had just been sitting. 'You look like the world is about to fall in.'

'It is,' said Jo. She pointed to her phone. 'I've just had a call from some fancy solicitor from London. It seems the families of the missing men have banded together, and he is their legal representative. If there aren't results soon, he will sue the department in general and me in particular for gross misconduct. He will call for an independent review body into the failings of Chichester Police.'

Jo leaned forward and placed her forehead against her desk, covering her head with her arms, in desperation. It didn't help. She couldn't protect herself. Missiles were being hurled at her from all directions and she had no answers.

CHAPTER 32

Even the ringing of the tip line couldn't pull Jo from her depression. In fact she could argue it had made it worse. But she did her best as she addressed the troops at the daily briefing.

'We're here today to help collate and sift the calls from the public with sightings of the missing. As you know there's been significant media interest. The trouble is, statistically, the sightings are often mistaken and rarely, but occasionally, deliberately made to mislead the investigators. I've worked with Sasha on a system and a means of grading and summarising the sightings, to assist prioritisation. We'll be logging each call on a missing persons database she's set up. There's a crib sheet for everyone for those calls. Please complete the form during the live call. Don't worry too much about your prose and spelling. I want concise information in the correct boxes to aid sorting and corroboration. I expect our band of brothers here to expand as the day goes on.

'But we can do this people. We've got this. The victims deserve our best work and we won't let them down. Will we?'

'No.' Some mumbled, some shook their heads, some

looked at the floor to avoid her eyes.

Oh, God, this was going down worse than she'd anticipated. She tried again. 'Come on, people,' she encouraged, walking backwards and forwards at the front of the room. 'Here at Chichester police station we're a great bunch of people. We've been up against it for a while, I know. But this force has integrity, honour, and a reputation for being one of the best in the constabulary. I know we have times when the press attack us. We feel some of the families hate us. But do you know what my father would say? Don't let the bastards grind you down.'

That produced a few titters.

'We know how good we are. Here's our chance to shine. So, as I said, we've got this. We won't let the victims down. Will we?'

'No!'

Jo looked around. Most had answered, but there were still a few stragglers who were non-committal.

'Will we?' she shouted, prowling the room, feeling like a UK Steve Jobs.

'NO!'

'That's better,' she grinned. 'Come on, let's do this.'

She clapped her troops and thankfully they joined in. The heavy atmosphere in the room had lifted and once more there was a feeling of hope. It was only a small chink in the wall that they were up against. But she'd take whatever she could get.

'Nice one,' said Byrd sidling up to her. 'Very Henry V.'

Jo smiled. 'Worked though, didn't it. A bit of, "Once more unto the breach" gets everyone, every time.'

As the day went on, the calls came in thick and fast. They had to add more extensions and more officers as they became overwhelmed by the volume of sightings. Jo pulled staff from wherever she could, to answer the calls and log the responses.

Then it was up to Sasha to do her thing with the data the officers collected. All sightings had to be recorded in the missing persons database. Sightings would be evaluated alongside other information gathered as part of the investigation, actions taken, and the rationale recorded.

As Jo flicked through the calls, she was starkly aware that assumptions should be avoided, and any uncorroborated details should be challenged to ensure enquiries were not based on inaccurate information. Sightings must be carefully managed to ensure that they were properly considered in the context of the overall investigation. The reliability of any sightings received should always be assessed and attempts made to corroborate the information.

On day three, the team managed to sit down and go through the results. There was a list of possible sightings and a list of any other missing persons cases that had similarities. They were looking for depressed, lonely, local men, last seen near Pagham or liked going there.

Had anyone called in saying that they'd seen person or persons like that while going about their daily business?

Any late-night dog walkers with information? People hiking in more remote parts of the region? Or day trippers and locals using the shingle beaches in the area, or even those visiting the sandy regions of the Witterings? There was always the holiday park. How many people from there had phoned in with information?

They couldn't believe the results. All those calls and all that data resulted in… precisely bugger all.

None of it had really helped. There was nothing that stood out. Nothing corroborated with other known facts about the missing. The one saving grace in the whole debacle was that at least they hadn't turned up any more victims and furthermore, Jo had done what was expected of her. But it was a bitter pill to swallow.

CHAPTER 33

Jo made her lonely way home that night. Byrd was off playing squash, or some such other very energetic sport. He'd asked if she'd wanted to go, but she'd declined, deciding she'd have an early night. But once home, she changed her mind. The weather was mild, the sun still up, perfect conditions for a run. Quickly changing her clothes, Jo grabbed water, her keys, phone, and ear buds. She was ready.

Pausing to push her valuables into a bum bag and clipping her water bottle to her belt, she caught sight of herself in the mirror in the hall.

But it wasn't her.

The woman reflected there had dark hair like Jo, but the locks were frazzled ringlets, kind of dreadlocks, but woven through with bits of colour. Flowers. Shells. Coral.

Jo staggered backwards and bumped into the opposite wall. Her skin was crawling. The woman exuded such an air of menace in her stare, that Jo found it hard to breathe. She was pinned to the wall by fear. But still she couldn't tear her eyes away from the apparition.

There was no one to help her. Byrd was gone. Her father was out. And where the fuck was Judith?

Now the woman was growing in size in the mirror. As though she were walking towards Jo. The nearer she got the bigger she got. Gone was her white shift dress. Gone was her slim body, arms and hands. All Jo could see was the woman's face. Piercing black pupils locked onto Jo's. The temperature in the flat plummeted.

The woman opened her mouth. Wider. And yet wider. Her jaw seemed to dislocate. Now the skin on her face stretched. The mouth was growing. Filling the whole of the mirror. Jo felt the apparition's hot fetid breath as it wormed its way out of the mirror and towards Jo. Strands of ectoplasm came from the mouth, feeling for their victim. There was no longer any glass stopping them. They moved independently, waving in the air, like hungry coral blindly searching for food. Seeking Jo. Getting nearer and nearer.

Jo couldn't breathe. Couldn't speak. And then in one desperate gasp she filled her lungs and screamed, 'Judith!'

The glass mirror broke. Large and small shards of glass blew outwards into the hall, aiming straight for Jo. She dropped to the floor, covered her head with her hands and waited out the storm of glass.

As the last pieces fell to the ground, Jo was left alone in her now silent flat.

Shaking with adrenaline and fear, she managed to get herself upright without sustaining any bad cuts. She stood amongst a confetti of glass for a moment, before turning and staggering into the bathroom. Peeling off her clothes, and shaking out her hair, she stepped into the shower. Turning on the taps, she stood under cold water, hoping to stem the blood running from the cuts on her arms and legs. The water swirled around her feet, coloured red by her blood. Turning the water to hot, Jo leant against the wall of the shower stall, slid down the tiled wall until she was sitting under the stream of water and cried.

CHAPTER 34

After last night's debacle Jo realised she had to talk to Byrd. Going in search of a decent cup of coffee, and not the watery brew at the station, seemed an ideal opportunity. Sitting opposite each other with large, steaming cups of flat white coffee in front of them, Jo looked pensive. Unsure as to how to start. But keeping the Kelpie a secret any longer wasn't an option.

Byrd unknowingly gave her an opening. 'You okay, Jo? You look miles away.'

'I was just thinking about the case.'

'What about it?'

'I know, um, I might know who, or what, is behind the disappearances.'

'Well considering the fact that we haven't got a real live human suspect, you must be talking about the what variety.'

Jo nodded. 'Some sort of Kelpie or water horse, evil spirit, something like that,' her words tailed off, not knowing how best to explain her experiences.

'Really?'

'Yes.'

'Alright. How do you know?'

'Um, I might have seen it.'

Byrd looked shocked, eyes widening, and he leaned over to grab her hand. 'What the...? When? Are you alright?'

Jo cringed. She knew the next bit wasn't going to go down well. 'Um, it all started when... Oh sod it! I've been going to a local stables. Helping with the horses, grooming, mucking out.'

Eddie puffed out a breath and withdrew his hand. 'You've been riding.' Resigned. Not a question. More of a statement.

Jo nodded. 'Along the beach that's all, more of a walk. A couple of them needed exercising.'

'So you did it just to help out?'

'Kind of. Sort of.'

He looked desperately sad that she would deliberately put herself in harm's way again. After the accident. After the coma. After all the recuperation. But then he seemed to gather himself and said, 'OK, putting that aside for a minute, what did you see?'

So Jo told him about the vision of the horse coming at her through the water. Rearing up. Nearly unseating her.

'A warning?'

'I reckon it was a threat. You know, showing off.'

'How do you mean?'

'Well, if it's a 'she' because of the young men disappearing, then she'd have no interest in me. She just wanted to let me know she was there. A challenge maybe? Throwing down of the gauntlet? But then...'

'Then what?'

With tears shining in her eyes, Jo confessed to seeing the Kelpie just before her car crash, hence the hoof marks in the bonnet. And then again in the mirror at her flat last night. 'She knows that I haven't stopped looking for her. That I didn't take her warnings seriously.'

'And this latest incident was in the flat? Last night?'

The whiteness of Eddie's face and the slight trembling of his hand told Jo that he wasn't happy about any of it.

'Dear God, Jo. I'm not sure I can handle this. Not something so close as to be in the flat. I... I need some air.'

He abruptly stood, scraping the chair away from him, nearly knocking it over. He grabbed it, banged it back down on four legs and then walked off. Jo remained seated, watching him leave the café, walking away from her. She wasn't sure what to make of his reaction. Whether to be upset, or just shrug and guess he'd be back soon enough. Once he'd got his head round it.

CHAPTER 35

Greta Fernholt opened the door to find a woman stood there, gazing at her coolly. She was very striking, her dark hair had white flashes in it at the front. The impression was of dark coloured, layered, flowing clothing and she had lots of gold bangles and necklaces. A gypsy.

'No thank you,' rasped Greta.

'No thank you to what?' The woman's voice was low with a slight eastern European accent.

'Lucky heather, or whatever it is that you're selling.'

'Oh well, if you don't want to know, it's your loss. I'll be off.'

As she turned and began to walk away, Greta's hand grabbed the woman's arm. 'Know what?'

The gypsy turned back. 'I have information about your son.'

Greta didn't trust the woman stood before her. But could she really not hear what she had to say? A pair of dark eyes looked indifferent. As though it didn't matter to her if Greta wanted to hear. Or not hear. 'But the police...'

'Have sent me,' she said.

Greta doubted that. But again, she couldn't be sure. 'Oh bugger it, come in,' and she beckoned the gypsy into her home. They sat at the small kitchen table.

'I've had expenses,' the woman said.

'Of course you have,' said Greta and reaching up to the top shelf of a cupboard pulled down a tin. She took £10 out of it and placed it in the woman's open palm.

Neither spoke.

'Jesus,' said Greta and withdrew another £10, which she placed on top of the first.

The money disappeared into the folds of the gypsy's clothing. Greta sat down opposite her and waited.

Then the gypsy's hand shot out and grabbed at Greta, who began to feel cold, as though the temperature in the room had suddenly dropped 10 degrees Celsius. Cold radiated from the gypsy's hand and began to spread up Greta's arm.

'He's in a very dark place.' The light in the kitchen dimmed, as though the sun had gone behind a bank of dark clouds. 'He's not alone.'

Greta whimpered. Her arm was as cold as ice and she began to shiver. She wished she'd never invited the woman into her home.

'He's beyond your grasp.'

Greta's eyes filled with tears. What the hell did that mean? 'But he's alive?'

The gypsy nodded. 'A prisoner.'

Then she let go of Greta, stood, and left the house without another word.

Greta began rubbing life back into her arm as the sun came out from behind the clouds and warmed up the kitchen.

'Stupid cow,' she mumbled to herself. That had made no sense whatsoever. Greta was still no nearer to finding her son and was now out of pocket to the tune of £20. Grabbing the tin and pulling off the lid, her worst fears were realised. She was skint. Rummaging in her handbag she found her mobile phone.

She paced the kitchen as she rang the Daily Post and was put through to the reporter who had written the piece on her missing son.

'You're not going to believe what's just happened,' she began. 'I'll give you an exclusive. But it'll cost you £1,000. In cash.'

CHAPTER 36

Jo took her time finishing her coffee and amused herself by watching the other customers. Men and women in suits joined young mothers and their children at the many tables. The air was potent with the smell of coffee and the chatter of small children. She gave a wistful smile at the normalcy of it. Ordinary people getting on with their ordinary lives. She longed for that. Craved it at times. But she was not normal. Never would be again. Her gift had seen to that. Jo scooped up the last of the foam in her cup with her spoon, swallowed it, then grabbed her bag. It was time to return to work. Eddie would either be there, or he wouldn't. The decision was his, not hers. All she could do was hope.

An hour later Byrd appeared at her office door. He gave her a lopsided grin, which she took to be an apology. But really, he had nothing to apologise for. It must be hard going out with a psychic, having to talk to a dead colleague and seeing things that no man ever wanted to see again. It was enough to make anybody shudder.

He just said one word. 'Osian?'

Jo nodded. 'Yes, I guess so. And Jill.'

'I'll arrange a meet.'

'Thanks, Byrd,' Jo offered her own lopsided grin. 'Look, I'm sorry,' she started, but was interrupted.

'Jo, you have nothing to apologise for. You didn't ask for this. Come to think of it, neither did I. But it is what it is. We'll deal with it, the best way we can. Together.'

That small speech threatened to be the undoing of her. It wasn't just the few words strung together. It was the meaning behind them. The love. Byrd had her back and she had his. She sniffed. Then grabbed her bag and ran for the Ladies. It didn't do to show emotion in the office.

Once the door had closed behind her with a soft thud, Jo looked in the mirror over the sink.

Then yelped.

'Judith! What the hell are you doing here?' she said in a stage whisper, glancing behind her to check the cubicles were empty. 'What is it with you lot and mirrors?'

Judith ignored Jo's question and said, 'I hear you had a visitor last night.'

'Yes, where the hell were you? Couldn't you stop her?'

'I wish,' said Judith. 'I'd been doing a good job of tracking her movements and keeping her away from you, but she gave me the slip. Sorry about that.'

'Oh, well that makes it alright then. You're sorry. Nice one.'

Jo knew her anger was taking over, but she couldn't help it. She'd been so bloody frightened. All alone in the flat, glass all over her, attacked by a malevolent supernatural being. She'd covered all the other mirrors in the flat and hardly slept a wink all night.

'We're going to need help with this one,' Judith said, changing the subject.

Jo instantly agreed. 'Are you sure that she took our missing men?'

'Absolutely.'

'Right. Byrd is arranging for us all to meet up. Me,

Eddie, Jill and Osian. We need to find a way forward.'

'Tell me about it. She's too strong for me, Jo. I can't do this on my own. Sorry.'

Jo was about to tell Judith that she had nothing to be sorry for, but abruptly her friend had gone.

The only thing reflected in the mirror was herself.

CHAPTER 37

'So I think we're dealing with a kind of mythical Kelpie.'

Jo had just finished summing up their problem with the being who they were fairly sure was behind the disappearance of 10 young men. It was more for Osian than Jill and Byrd, who were both working the cases with Jo. They were all sitting in Jo's flat, Jo and Byrd drinking wine, Jill and Osian on soft drinks as they were driving.

She then went on to tell them about her encounter with the being whilst riding along the shore.

'So you really believe it's a mythical Kelpie?' repeated Jill. 'What the hell is one of those?'

'Ah,' said Jo. 'Well, there are many Scottish myths and legends about kelpies. Kelpies are also referred to as water kelpies because they live most of their lives in the water. The name originated in Scotland to describe the shape-shifting water spirits inhabiting the lochs, rivers, and streams. Kelpies commonly appear looking like a powerful black horse, but they can also take on the form of a human. Sometimes those forms combine to create a human with hooves for feet, which is why people have compared Kelpies to the devil. But I think our Kelpie is more like the Mermaid of Padstow.'

'Okay,' grinned Byrd. 'I'll bite. Who's she?'

Jo gook a gulp of her wine and soda before continuing. 'In years gone by, Padstow was an important port as it was a natural safe haven on an otherwise rocky coast. However, over the years the river mouth has become so choked up with drifting sand as to be more or less useless to anything but small craft. In the past it had been deep enough for even the largest of vessels and was under the care of a merry maid.'

'In other words a mermaid?' asked Jill.

'Exactly,' replied Jo. 'One day, for reasons that are not clear, she was shot by a sailor from a visiting boat. She dived for a moment but then re-appeared to make a vow. Raising her right hand she swore the harbour would be from that day forth desolate, and always would be. Shortly after, a storm blew up wrecking several ships and throwing up the huge sandbank known as the Doom Bar. Since then the sandbank has caused a great number of ships to flounder through the centuries.'

'I seem to remember tales of mermaids luring men to her watery home under the sea,' said Jill. 'I went to Cornwall on holiday once and became fascinated by the tales.'

'Come on then,' said Osian to Jill, who seemed to be enjoying himself hugely. 'Don't keep us in suspense. What's their stories?'

'In one of several versions of the tale, the mermaid Morveren enjoyed sitting on a rock at Hawker's Cove. Falling in love with a local man named Mathew, Morveren was drawn to the church by his beautiful voice and would dress as a human and listen from the back of the church. Every night at evensong the mermaid would come to hear him, until one night as Mathew sang a particularly lovely verse, Morveren let out a tiny sigh. Although the sigh was as quiet as a whisper, Mathew stopped and turned to look at her. Morveren's eyes were shining, and the net had slipped from her head. Her hair was wet and gleaming. It was love at first sight.'

'Wow,' said Osian, looking at Jill in exactly the same way as the mermaid had looked at Mathew.

She grinned, then continued, 'But the mermaid was frightened and made her way back to the sea with Mathew in pursuit. In her haste to get back to the sea Morveren became tangled in her dress and tripped. Mathew saw the tip of her fish tail poking out from beneath the dress. 'I cannot stay. I am a sea creature and must go back where I belong,' she said. But it didn't matter to him. 'Then I will go with ye. For with ye is where I belong,' said Mathew. With that he picked up Morveren and ran into the sea, never to be seen by the village folk again. However that didn't mean they never heard him. He would sing soft and high if the day was to be fair, deep and low if the seas were to be rough. From his songs, the fishermen of Zennor knew when it was safe to put to sea, and when it was wise to anchor up and stay snug at home.'

Jo nodded. 'There are lots of stories that tell of mermaids who allegedly sit on a rock and sing whilst combing their hair, in an effort to lure local fishermen to a watery grave,' she said. 'Either way, whichever legend is true, I believe we're dealing with someone or something who managed to lure our 10 young men into the sea.'

That seemed to sober up the group. Gone was the excitement of telling Halloween tales. They weren't kids telling ghost stories under a sheet with a torch. This was serious business.

Osian became quiet. Thoughtful. 'There's something there...' he said. 'Someone. I'm sure an elderly priest had a reputation for driving out evil spirits. I just can't place when and where at the moment. I must have it noted somewhere.'

He stood to leave.

'Do you want to go for a drink on the way home?' Jill asked him.

But Osian seemed distracted. 'Sorry, love, I must find him. I need to unravel this knotty problem. It's bugging me, this priest. I'm busy in the cathedral tomorrow, so tonight's the only chance I'll have.'

'Maybe tomorrow night?'

Osian nodded, said his farewells, and walked off.

Jo could see Jill was upset. 'Don't worry, Jill. Osian's just preoccupied. It's nothing more than that, I'm sure.'

'Anyway,' said Byrd. 'Let's all call it a night. There's nothing more we can do now. What we need is help and hopefully Osian can provide that soon.'

CHAPTER 38

All the way home, Osian worried about their latest case. All those young men. It didn't bear thinking about. All those grieving families. Perhaps he could visit with some, or all of them. Try and bring them some comfort. But, of course, he knew full well that some wouldn't welcome his visit. Would see it as an intrusion. Not many people these days seemed to have a predilection for religion.

So in that case, maybe the best way was to help Jill, Jo, and Byrd to find their mythical beast. And the key to that was the one thing he couldn't remember! He banged his hand on the steering wheel in frustration. The one thing he could do to help… and he couldn't remember.

Arriving home, which was in clerical housing near the Cathedral, he parked his yellow Fiat 500. Some saw it as a whimsical purchase, or one designed to get people to smile. Osian had it for sentimental reasons. It was his mother's old car. When she'd died earlier that year, it was the only thing of hers he really wanted. Every time he drove it, he remembered a different part of her life, her love, her commitment to God and her family. And that made him smile and brought him comfort.

Climbing the stairs to his apartment, he decided to

make a cup of tea and then start looking. He felt the information the elderly priest may have could be vital to their quest. He didn't know how he knew this, but he felt it in his heart.

As he stood in the kitchen waiting for the kettle to boil, which sounded unnaturally loud in the silent, empty flat, he wished he'd asked Jill to come back with him. He knew he must stop thinking about their relationship as an either - or thing. As in I'll either look for the priest, or I'll see you. She could have come back with him. Let's face it, her mere presence would have helped. Helped ground him. Helped encourage him to do his best. The flat was just too empty and lonely without her.

Taking his tea to his desk, Osian started. This had to be done. With or without Jill. Osian opened each drawer in turn. Examined each file and document. His desk had three drawers on each side and a long thin one just under the top. None of the seven contained the information he was seeking.

Stifling a yawn, he saw it was approaching midnight. There was nothing more to be done that night. His other papers were in the loft and he wasn't going to start getting down boxes and disturbing his neighbours. It was time for bed. Dragging himself off to the bathroom, he had a quick wash and cleaned his teeth, then fell into bed.

He drifted off to sleep, his mind still working away at the knotty problem of the mysterious priest, when he suddenly sat bolt upright. He'd been having a dream. Father Jacob had come to him. Finally Osian had remembered the old man's name and where he was. The Father had had a reputation for driving out evil spirits, but it was very draining work, which he gave up upon his retirement. He was in a church nursing home in Worthing. Osian had the strong feeling that Father Jacob was waiting for him and so vowed to go to see him the following evening.

CHAPTER 39

The next morning Jo was walking past Sykes' office. She hoped he wouldn't notice her, but no such luck. He called out, 'Jo!'.

She turned and saw he was waiving a piece of paper around and beckoning to her.

'Morning, Sir,' she said as cheerfully as she could manage. Even though there was nothing cheerful about Sykes. Ever. Nor did it look like that day was going to be any different.

'Jo,' he said, but not asking her to sit. 'I've had a very unfortunate letter, I'm afraid.'

Jo couldn't see what that had to do with her but played along. 'About what, Sir?'

'You.'

Oh shit. Here we go, she thought.

'From the solicitor representing the families of the missing men.'

Double shit.

'It says that unless some progress is made, they will have no option but to take further action.'

'Meaning?' Jo managed, although she was feeling rather faint.

'Meaning a shit storm at the least. Or demotion at the worst.'

'Demotion?' Jo couldn't believe what she was hearing. Was this true? Or just another Sykes bullying tactic?

He seemed to have read her thoughts when he said, 'This is no idle threat, Jo. Families have complained about you and quite frankly I agree with them. Your investigation to date is not good enough and I strongly urge you to try harder and do better. How many more times do I have to tell you that we need a result on this one?'

Jo moved slightly backward so she could lean against the wall of Sykes' office. She hoped he wouldn't notice, but she desperately needed a prop.

'I'm afraid you're never going to get far in the force if you don't. You can't always rely on your father's reputation to keep you in the force. Nor his friends in high places. You must do it on your own merit. And at the moment you're severely lacking. Do I make myself clear?'

'Yes, Sir,' said Jo, biting her tongue. She really wanted to tell him how unfair the criticism was. That this had all started with her investigating the case of a missing young man, Colin, and had spiralled out of control from there.

The other nine missing men were cold cases, mostly before Jo joined Chichester CID. But Sykes was clearly in no mood to be reminded of those facts. He was an evil man who relished having Jo under his control. But it wouldn't last forever. They'd soon break this case wide open.

But this time she needed a perpetrator to arrest and charge. Or at the very least, the body of one. She couldn't get away with mystical creatures who disappeared for much longer.

Thankfully, Jo was dismissed without a further tongue

lashing. As she ran down the stairs, she vowed never to visit the 5th floor again and get inadvertently caught in Sykes' sticky web.

CHAPTER 40

First thing the next morning, Osian put in a telephone call to the Church Pensions Board care home, Kirkwood House in Worthing.

His call was answered by a deep throated woman, who managed to sound full of life just by answering the telephone. 'Kirkwood House, how may I help you?'

'Good morning,' Osian said. 'My name is Father Osian Price and I wondered if Father Jacob was still with you?' Osian didn't dare ask if the elderly priest had died.

'Oh yes, he's alive and kicking, very much so.'

'I was hoping to visit later today. Would that be possible?'

'Of course. He loves having visitors, but you must be careful not to over-tire him.'

'I understand.'

'Have you been here before?'

'No, no I've not.'

'In that case, I'll have to take your name, address and telephone number now. I'll also call you back sometime today, just to confirm you are who you say you are. Where are you based, Father Osian?'

Osian gave her all the relevant information.

'Thank you, I'll tell Father Jacob, he'll be waiting for your visit.'

The care home in Worthing looked more like an old church than a nursing home. All Victorian red brick and arched windows, it was easy to see that the building had ecclesiastical leanings. It was only a short walk from the seafront in Worthing and the terrain was level and the pavements wide.

Osian watched the swooping gulls before going in. They were so free, up there in the air. But then he saw another group, squabbling. Fighting over scraps left behind by the tourists. Fish and chip paper was being thrown around as the gulls tried to get to the prize inside.

Ah well, thought Osian. Maybe they weren't that free and easy after all. Their life seemed to mirror that of humans, where petty squabbles and fights abounded.

He was greeted at the desk by a mature woman, he supposed you could call her. She was rather glamorous and had the air of a Blackpool landlady. Chatty, vivacious, and dressed to kill. She flashed her white teeth and ample bosom at him as she leaned forward and pointed in the direction Osian should take.

'Father Jacob is waiting for you in his room.'

Osian thanked her and was glad to escape her clutches. He only hoped she wouldn't be there when he left. He was beginning to feel like a spider in her web. A spider that ate the male after mating.

Father Jacob answered Osian's knock with a frail, 'Come in.'

When Osian entered the room, the elderly priest was sitting in a wheelchair, a blanket over his lap. The television was burbling away to itself in a corner of the room.

'Come in, come in,' he called. 'I've been waiting for you. Father Price isn't it?'

'That's correct, Sir,' said Osian walking closer. 'Thank you for agreeing to meet me.'

'Glad to, my boy,' he replied. 'Don't get so many visitors these days, you know? How can I help? The girls said you had a thorny problem for me.'

'First of all, could I just ask, for clarification, um… were you a…' Osian realised he was hesitant to come out with the term he was looking for. Oh well, he thought. Here goes. 'A bit of a psychic,' Osian said.

Father Jacob grinned. 'Yes, I was a psychic priest, I suppose you could call me. All glittering powers and such, when I was much younger, in the swinging 60's and whatever the 70's were supposed to be.'

'Do you mean exorcisms?'

'Sometimes, but more than that. More psychic visions, which didn't make much sense at the time, but became clear eventually, depending upon what the Lord was trying to tell me.'

'So you believe they all came from God?'

'I used to think so, yes.'

'And now?'

Suddenly the old man grabbed Osian's hand with a surprisingly crushing grip and wouldn't let go. His head tipped backwards, and his eyes rolled. His mouth gaped open and the two men stayed locked together for a couple of minutes. Osian kept quiet and let the old man do his thing. When he came to, he said something unexpected. 'You too can have this gift. The Lord is willing to give it to you, but you have to believe.'

Osian frowned. 'But I do believe.'

He thought that an odd question coming from Father Jacob. After all, Osian was a member of the clerical team at Chichester Cathedral.

'Ah, but do you believe enough? Do you believe with all your heart and soul?'

Father Jacob's words were disconcerting.

'There is no doubting God's word, nor his world. If you search your soul and decide you are with God, then he will come to your aid. And the aid of your three friends. Now you'll have to forgive me, I find this very draining. Perhaps you'd press the call button for one of the girls. I'd like to go to bed with a cup of tea.'

'Of course, thank you for sharing that with me, Father Jacob.'

The old man nodded. As Osian reached the door, Father Jacob called, 'Oh, and tell Jo that Judith will be back. She hasn't deserted you all. You will see her again.'

CHAPTER 41

Osian was glad to be out of the nursing home and back in his car. He was shaken by the encounter with Father Jacob, who had just mentioned Osian's three close friends and the work they did, insinuating that God would help them, but only if Osian believed. That was creepy enough, as Osian had told Father Jacob nothing of their current quest. Not even that there were three other people involved.

But the worst thing?

Talking about Jo and Judith in particular. How the hell did he know about them? And the personal message Judith had for Jo. What was that all about? If Judith had a message for Jo, she was quite capable of telling her herself! Was it just for validation? Proof that Father Jacob was able to communicate with the other side? A demonstration, just so Osian would believe him?

It was clear Father Jacob had seen a lot of Osian's life in a few short moments when he'd grabbed his arm. And the way the old man's eyes had rolled back in his head. The sight of the whites of his eyes filling the space between the lids where his pupils should have been, completely gave him the creeps. It was like something out of a horror movie. He was sure Father Jacob had had a vision right in front of him!

Osian had to admit he was scared. His world had been rocked and it sounded as if he may be found wanting. What was it the old man had said? You must believe with all your heart in God. Osian always thought he did. But Father Jacob appeared to be calling that faith into question. He was making Osian examine his work and his faith like no other had done. He'd love to talk it over with Jill, but she was busy with the case. Maybe he could persuade her to have a drink later that evening. Surely, she wouldn't be working around the clock.

The irony was, of course, that he now knew how Jill had felt yesterday. When he'd dismissed her out of hand. Been so focused on his work that he'd felt there wasn't room for Jill to join him. He knew different now. At least now that the boot was on the other foot as it were. He sighed. Relationships were so hard. And right about now he had problems with two of them. One, his relationship with God and two, his relationship with Jill.

He didn't want to lose either. But could he keep both?

CHAPTER 42

As he suspected, Jill had worked late last night and Osian had spent a second lonely evening. He was beginning to think that it served him right. That God was giving him a taste of his own medicine. What was the line? Do unto others as you would have them do unto you. A command based on the words of Jesus in the Sermon on the Mount: "All things whatsoever ye would that men should do to you, do ye even so to them." He must be less cavalier in his dealings with his girlfriend.

He stopped with a slice of toast halfway to his mouth. Girlfriend. Is that what Jill was? She was certainly his best friend with benefits. Not that they had slept together. But they enjoyed each other's company a great deal, kissed and cuddled and told each other everything. So yes, he guessed she was his girlfriend. He wondered if that was how Jill saw their relationship. Then an image of her smiling up at him flashed into his head. Of course Jill saw herself as his girlfriend. He'd seen the way she looked at him, a smile playing across her lips, her eyes shining, the feel of her hand tucked into the crook of his elbow.

And then he saw himself, smiling down on her, in the same way.

What was the popular expression? Oh yes, wake up and smell the coffee. And he didn't mean the enticing vapours emanating from his cafetiere on the kitchen table next to him. He really had to do something to put their relationship on a more permanent footing. But what? That was too tricky a knot to unpick this morning. Anyway, to work. Osian grabbed his mobile and rang Kirkwood House. He did need to clarify things with Father Jacob. He walked around his kitchen as he waited for Blackpool Landlady. She answered. But her cheerful disposition was gone. She sounded muted, flat, and Osian wondered what on earth was wrong.

'Good morning,' he called cheerfully. 'Father Price here, is it possible to come and see Father Jacob again today? Sometime in the afternoon perhaps?'

Now she sniffed. Actually sniffed. Maybe she had a cold.

'I'm so sorry, Father,' she said. 'But no that won't be possible.'

Deflated, Osian said, 'Oh, I see,' even though he didn't. 'Perhaps tomorrow?'

She sniffed again, then stifled a sob. 'I'm sorry, Father, but Father Jacob died in the early hours of this morning.'

Osian sat. 'Died?' he managed weakly.

'Umm... He had a heart attack, just this morning.'

Osian wondered why God was testing him in this way. First offering a helping hand in the form of Father Jacob and then taking it away again.

'Do,' Osian cleared his throat which was constricted, then managed, 'Do you want me to come over and bless his body.'

'Very kind, but no, one of the others has done that.'

'Oh yes, yes of course.'

Osian had completely forgotten that Father Jacob lived... had lived... in a church nursing home. Osian had no more cards left to play. He was on his own. God was extracting his revenge for Osian's lack of faith.

'But if you could come over?'

'Pardon?'

'Father Jacob left a message for you last night.'

'Oh yes?' Osian held his breath.

'There's a box and an envelope for you. He was most insistent that you have it as soon as possible. Wouldn't sleep until the girls had promised to make sure it got to you, apparently.'

Osian rose and began pacing. 'A box and an envelope, you said?'

'Yes.'

Osian looked at his watch. 9 am. He had choir practice at 11am, but he was free until then. 'I'm on my way,' he said, had a final mouthful of coffee, grabbed his keys, and ran.

CHAPTER 43

Jo was queuing up for coffee that morning. It was her turn for the morning brew, as no one could face the awful machine coffee early in the morning. Happily cocooned in a warm shop with the sound of the large coffee machines working at full throttle, the enticing aromas of fresh coffee, fresh pastries and hot paninis were making her stomach rumble. She gazed around and saw a paper left on an empty table. Reaching for it, she began flicking through it while she waited.

"Psychic gypsy helps police!" screamed a headline on page three. Jo smiled to herself, yet another sensational non-story, she expected. The Daily Post was always full of them. Jo took them with a pinch of salt. It reminded her of the Daily Examiner in the USA. Lurid headlines with little substance in the story.

Jo decided to read on, hoping for a good laugh she could have with the others when she got into the office.

There was a sketch accompanying the article, which was supposedly of the gypsy. Then a picture of Greta Fernholt. And finally a picture of Jo. She closed her eyes, not wanting to believe what she'd just seen. But when she opened them, the article was still there. Jo took a deep breath, closed the paper, tucked it under her arm and ran out of the shop to a chorus of shouts.

'Oy, come back, your coffees are ready.'

'You can't take the paper, it's mine!'

'Stop that thief!'

Jo took no notice of any of them and ran all the way to the police station.

She threw the newspaper on Byrd's desk, then rang Liam Statham demanding that he come to her office at once.

'Bloody hell, Jo,' Byrd said from her office door, the paper open in his hands.

'I know,' said Jo. 'Just when you think things can't get any worse. They do.'

They looked up at the sound of running feet and a male voice saying, 'Sorry. Sorry. Excuse me,' as Liam skidded to a halt outside Jo's door.

'Guv?' he asked.

Silently Byrd handed him the paper, opened to page three. As he read, Liam's face turned white, his eyes wide and staring. 'Oh, God,' he managed.

'I suggest you go and make some calls, then meet us outside Detective Chief Inspector Sykes' office in 15 minutes,' said Jo, her voice as cold as her mood.

Liam seemed incapable of speech, his mouth opening and closing. Giving up trying to speak, he nodded to Jo instead, turned and ran.

To Liam's credit, he was there as requested, on time and hopping from one foot to another as the three of them waited outside Sykes' door. They hadn't been summoned but had turned up voluntarily. However, it was clear Sykes was well aware of the offending article. He was in his office with the Chief Superintendent. Yet again. On the desk Jo could see an open copy of the Daily Post.

The door opened and all three were called in. The

Chief Superintendent was sitting in Sykes' chair and Sykes was standing next to it. The three of them lined up in front of the desk.

'For God's sake, Jo,' the Chief Supt began. 'Not again!' he shook his head. 'Why is it that trouble seems to follow you around?'

Jo had no answer to that question, so stayed silent. Jo, Byrd, and Liam were standing stiffly side by side, waiting for the axe to fall, wondering which one of them was for the chop. Or maybe it was to be all three of them.

'Let's start with you, Sergeant Statham. What have you got to say about this article, eh?'

'It wasn't me!' Liam managed to blurt.

'I never said it was, Sergeant. I asked what you knew about it?'

'Oh, right, sorry, Sir.'

Jo listened as Liam had to admit that he'd known about the article, as he was telephoned by the reporter before the paper went to press, asking for a quote from the police. Liam had declined to comment. But he hadn't told anyone and had hoped the paper wouldn't actually publish the story.

'Dear God, Statham. Didn't you learn anything from those expensive courses we sent you on?' The Chief Supt rubbed a hand across his face and then, for good measure, shook his head. 'That's just not good enough. We should all have been alerted about this possible story.'

'Sorry, Sir,' Liam mumbled, hanging his head, and studying his shoes like a recalcitrant schoolboy caught fighting in the playground and summoned to the headmaster's office.

'So, yet another failing of the Press Office.'

No one said anything to that.

'Jo, did you have any dealings with the Daily Post about this?'

She held her head high. 'No, Sir.'

'Or Greta Fernholt?'

Again, an emphatic, 'No, Sir.'

'Byrd?'

Eddie looked startled at being asked a question. 'No, Sir!' he said, appearing indignant at the mere thought of it.

'Statham!'

The Sergeant looked up, startled.

'Did you get any indication from The Post as to who their source was?'

'Not in so many words, Sir.'

'Well, what did you get?'

'Oh, sorry. The journalist wouldn't give up his source but hinted it may have been Greta Fernholt herself and that she was being paid for the interview. Obviously, I have no way of knowing if that's the truth, Sir. But it's what I suspect.'

'Well, perhaps now you have had hands on experience of how slippery the press can be, you realise that the position in the Press Office is not a cushy number. There are repercussions every time you get something wrong. Serious repercussions.'

'Yes, Sir. Sorry, Sir.'

'Very well. Issue a complete denial of the story. Understood?'

'Yes, Sir.'

'Right. I'm satisfied that there was no leak. This time. Go away, the lot of you.'

As they left the office, and passed by the windows into Sykes' lair, Jo could see Sykes going red as the Chief Supt appeared to turn his wrath on their boss.

Liam fled for the lift and Jo and Eddie took the stairs. Halfway down, her legs wobbly, she stopped.

'You OK?'

She nodded. 'Yes. I just need a minute.' Looking up at him she continued, 'Thank God this time it wasn't anything to do with us. But I still believe we are on borrowed time and shit like this doesn't help. We must crack this case, Byrd. And fast.'

CHAPTER 44

Once in Worthing, Osian navigated the one-way system and soon arrived at Kirkwood House. He sat in the car for a few minutes, listening to the tick, tick, of the cooling engine as he fought to bring his breathing under control. What on earth could Father Jacob have left him that was so urgent? But he had to turn his mind away from that and calm down. Taking measured breaths he managed to stop his hands shaking, then climbed out of the car.

As he went through the doors of the nursing home, Blackpool Landlady was there behind the reception desk. He saw a name plaque he'd not noticed before. Maria Pool.

She looked up. 'Oh, Father Price. Thank you for coming.' Her eyes were red and swollen and she had developed a syncopated sniff.

'I'm so sorry for your loss, Ms Pool.'

'Thank you. Very kind. Here it is. From Father Jacob.'

From underneath the reception desk Ms Pool pulled out a shoe box with an envelope on top.

Osian took it and thanked her profusely. There being nothing else to say, he turned and walked back to his car. Once inside his vehicle he looked at the box. A shoe box.

Surely Father Price hadn't left him a pair of leather brogues? Osian's plan had been to return home before he opened his very own Pandora's Box, but found he couldn't wait. His fingers itched to open the lid. His eyes widened at the thought of what secrets the box held.

He held his breath. He eased the lid off. Inside, nestled in tissue paper, was a revolver. An old-fashioned affair with a revolving cylinder and hammer. It made Osian think of the wild west, and the phrase, 'Hi Ho, Silver!' flashed through his mind, making him smile at the remembered series he'd enjoyed watching at the Saturday morning pictures when he was a boy. Only this was nothing like the dull, serviceable weapons he was used to seeing the cowboys brandishing. The barrel looked like burnished silver, with ivory panels on the grip. They were both highly decorated. With one strange looking bullet by the side of it. Not that Osian knew much about guns or bullets. Osian frowned. He didn't understand.

He tore the envelope open and extracted a single sheet of writing paper, folded in half. He laid it flat on top of the shoe box.

The letter read:

Father Price,
This is what you need.
But I only have one bullet left.
You must not miss.
Before you fire the bullet, you must ask yourself
do you really believe?
And if so, do you believe enough?

CHAPTER 45

That evening, the despondent four met to discuss what to do next. Sat in Osian's empty office in the Cathedral, no one really had any idea. Jo sighed. She was finding it hard to dispel her glum mood which was a hangover from the meeting she'd had with Sykes and the Chief Supt, about the psychic gypsy debacle.

She tried to rally herself and her troops by saying, 'Let's tell each other what we know so far and then brainstorm what we can do about it.'

'Alright,' said Osian. 'I'll go first.'

He walked over to his desk and pulled the shoe box out of the deep bottom drawer. He firstly told them about his visit to the old priest, and then about the gift left by him.'

'What was it, this gift?' said Jill, huge eyed.

'This.'

Like a conjurer he opened the lid with and flourish and passed the box around so they could each see the gun and the bullet.

'It's beautiful,' said Jill. 'Look at all that engraving. What does it mean? Has anyone ever seen a gun like this before?'

They all shook their heads.

'The trouble is,' said Osian. 'I've no idea what to do with it, or why he gave it to me. And this bullet doesn't look like any bullet I've ever seen. Not that I'm an expert, I know. But still…'

Jo stared at the gun, nestling it its tissue paper. 'I might know,' she said in a small voice, captivated by the sight of the gun and bullet.

'Really?' said Byrd.

Jo nodded. 'The myths tell that the way to kill a Kelpie is with a silver bullet. That's what the bullet must be made of.'

Byrd frowned. 'But how do we know? Really know?'

'We have to have faith.'

Byrd turned to Osian. 'In what?'

'Whatever works for you. For me, it's God, for you good against evil, I guess. Justice.'

Byrd thought for a minute, then nodded. 'I see what you mean.'

Jo said, 'I believe in things that I don't necessarily understand.'

'Like?'

'Like the afterlife, I guess. I believe in Judith.'

Osian turned to Jill. 'How about you?'

Jill shook her head. 'I don't know. I haven't had the experiences that Jo and Byrd have had, nor the unshakable faith that you have.'

'What do you believe in then?' asked Osian. 'If not God?'

'You,' she answered without hesitation. 'I believe in you.'

Jo watched as a smile spread over Osian's face and he reached out and grabbed Jill's hand. 'That's the nicest thing anyone's ever said to me.'

As Jill blushed, Jo decided to bring the conversation back around to the here and now. 'OK, so now we all believe in something, to one extent or another, we need to confront this bloody Kelpie. But when? And where? Any ideas?'

'Pagham beach would be a good start,' said Byrd.

'But how will we know when to go to the beach?' said Jill.

'Perhaps we should all think on that,' said Jo. 'If anyone has any good ideas, let the others know. But I've had enough for one day.' Jo caught Byrd's eye.

'Me too,' Byrd agreed. 'Bye you two,' he said to Osian and Jill, and followed Jo out of the door.

CHAPTER 46

The following morning, neither Jo nor Byrd had come up with any idea as to when they should go to Pagham beach. She wandered over to Sasha's desk to see if the girl could help Jo decide when the best time would be to confront the Kelpie. Sasha was always a mine of information and Jo was keeping her fingers crossed that she'd be able to help. Without telling Sasha the reason why Jo needed the information, of course.

'Sasha, have you come across any other correlations between the missing men, apart from the obvious gender, age, etc?'

'Of course,' replied the girl. 'How many do you want?'

'Um…' Sasha never ceased to amaze Jo. She always had lots of information at her fingertips but didn't necessarily share it. Not because she didn't want to, but because she just assumed everyone else had noticed the connections as well and not just her. She had an analytical mind when it came to data but didn't have the detective's flair in deciding how best to use it.

Sasha sighed. 'Well we have gender, age, hair colour, single/married/girlfriend, work or school. Then of course there's the timing.'

Jo jumped on that one. 'Timing? What about it?'

'All the men vanished during a full moon.'

'A full moon?' Jo was confused. A full moon was normally associated with the paranormal, but myths and legends leaned towards werewolves and the full moon. Nothing to do with kelpies that Jo knew of. But hey, she'd take what she could from it.

'That's what I said.' Sasha looked at Jo. A look that said why was she repeating what Sasha had just said.

'When's the next one?'

'The next what? Disappearance or full moon?'

Of course, Jo must remember that Sasha wasn't being obtuse, just literal. 'The next full moon.'

'That's easy. Tonight is a full moon. In fact, it's a Hunter's Moon.'

That sounded perfect. Just what she'd been hoping for. Jo wanted to kiss the girl, but refrained from acting rashly, so she mumbled her thanks and rushed to her office. Grabbing her mobile, Jo texted the others. "It's tonight. Meet at Pagham Beach 9pm. I'll explain then."

Jo pulled up in her newly mended, red Mini Clubman, to see that the others were there before her. Byrd was just getting out of his car and Jill and Osian were standing on the pebble beach, looking out to sea. They looked small against the vastness of the water stretching to the horizon. High clouds were forming, piling on top of each other, some white and some grey. But it was the encroaching black clouds that formed an ominous background, clearly lit by the light from the full moon. As Jo walked towards the water, the huge moon hung in the sky in front of her, it's beams forming a path across the sea towards them. Would this be the path the Kelpie would take? The thought of confronting the apparition that had appeared to Jo a month or so ago, filled her with fear. She still remembered the raging being rising out of the sea. A horse, yet not a horse, who turned into an attractive young woman, who was anything but.

Jo thought of the encounters they'd previously had. First, Anubis the God of Death, in that awful torture chamber that reeked of blood. Then Odin, the God of War, who killed so many and for what? He was hardly going to achieve world domination. Yet Jo still felt each death keenly. And the Watcher. She mustn't forget him. It took the five of them to drive the fallen angel back into hell where he belonged. Would the four of them be strong enough to kill the Kelpie? Only time would tell.

Jo looked at her motley band of warriors. Jill looked apprehensive. Osian pensive, clutching the box from Father Jacob in his hands. Byrd looked determined. Catching Jo's eye he managed a lopsided grin. Only Judith was missing. Jo hoped they wouldn't have to deal with the Kelpie on their own. She fervently hoped that Judith would appear at the crucial moment.

No one spoke. They lined up, staring at the sea. Scanning the waves and horizon for any movement. But all was calm, and Jo could hear the chink of cleats on the boat masts. Then there was nothing. It was as though they were in a vacuum. No noise. No disturbance. As one, they walked forwards and stopped a few feet from the lapping waves.

'Are you sure this is….?'

Jill didn't get to finish her question, as suddenly rearing up out of the water, rose the Kelpie and grabbed Jill in its vile mouth, dragging her through the shallows into deeper water. Once there, it seemed to play with her, shaking her from side to side like a dog playing with a toy.

'Jill!' screamed Osian and made to follow the Kelpie into the sea.

A horrified Jo shouted to him, 'Stop! You can't go, you have the gun and the bullet.' She grabbed at Osian's arm and yanked him back.

'But Jill! Oh God, Jill!'

Jo was just about to tell him it was alright, she would go, when she heard splashing. Turning back to the sea, she saw Byrd had charged into the churning water. 'Byrd! Come back!'

'You stay with Osian,' he yelled. 'Help him shoot the bloody thing.'

As Byrd charged into the water, the beast spotted him. With one giant shake of its head, it threw Jill away. Her body flew over the water, as soft and bedraggled as a rag doll. Byrd changed direction towards Jill as the Kelpie reared up onto its hind legs, screaming and neighing.

Lightening split the sky with its jagged beam of electrical energy and the thrashing of the horse's tail sounded like thunder. The noise echoed around the beach and seemed to be the signal the oppressive black clouds were waiting for, as driving rain fell. It hit Jo's head and face with stinging drops. Within seconds she was drenched.

'Take the shot, Osian!' Jo shouted against the wind and driving rain, cupping her mouth to direct her voice. 'Take the bloody shot!'

CHAPTER 47

Osian was struggling to remain calm. His eyes kept being pulled away from the Kelpie towards Jill. She was floating motionless in the sea as Byrd desperately tried to get to her. Osian could see him fighting the wind, rain, and the waves to save his friend. As he watched Jill's motionless body bobbing in the waves, he asked himself what Jill was to him. Jill was his what? Afraid to have that conversation with himself again, he pulled his eyes back towards the Kelpie.

By now the Kelpie was apoplectic at being denied her prize. She was constantly moving, hooves pawing at the waves, shaking her head from side to side. As he looked along the gun sights, he fancied he could see into her hate filled eyes. And that the Kelpie could see into his terrified ones. She mustn't see that Osian was afraid. Afraid for Jill and the others, but also afraid for his own life. He had no idea if shooting the Kelpie would work, or just make her madder.

Jo was screaming at him to take the shot, but his hands were shaking he was that bloody scared. Drops of rain dripped from his wet hair into his eyes, making them sting. The weather was definitely not helping.

By now, Byrd had reached Jill and taken her in his arms. They were still being threatened by the Kelpie, but somehow, she couldn't seem to reach them. It was as though they had a protective bubble around them. That was good enough for Osian. Knowing Jill was being protected meant that at last he could concentrate on killing the Kelpie.

Jo was shouting again, but her words were snatched away by the wind and buried by the thunderous sounds of the Kelpie thrashing its tail against the water in frustration.

Osian took one deep breath to steady himself, but doubt kept creeping into his mind. He wasn't at all sure he could take the shot and kill the Kelpie. But he had to, to save Jill. Then Father Jacob's questions came to mind.

'Do you believe enough? Do you believe with all your heart and soul?'

'Yes,' answered Osian. 'Yes, I do.'

He placed the shot in God's hands. He called on God to help him, to send his bullet straight and true, to kill the evil spirit. To watch over this warrior, battling evil in God's name.

The Kelpie reared once more.

As a bolt of lightning struck the beach, Osian shot it with the silver bullet.

CHAPTER 48

The crack of the shot echoed around Pagham beach, loud enough to wake the dead. Osian's ears were ringing, but he concentrated on the Kelpie. As the bullet hit it, the horse fell backwards into the sea and disappeared under the waves, but had the silver bullet done its job? Would the legend hold true? Could the Kelpie really be killed with a silver bullet?

He scanned the sea but could find neither sight nor sound of it. Mercifully, the thunderous thrashing of the horse's tail had stopped, and the beach became eerily quiet. The rain stopped and as Osian looked up, the dark clouds were breaking up and drifting away. The only sound was the soft lapping of the waves.

Byrd splashed out of the shallows and laid Jill tenderly on the beach. Osian was immediately at her side, kneeling on the pebbles, ignoring the pain in his knees from the stones. He began rubbing her limbs, holding a limp hand, and imploring her to wake up. There was no response. She felt so very cold, so he stripped off his jacket and laid it on her. It was wet through, of course, but being waterproof the inside was still dry and was warm from the heat from his body.

Taking her head in his hands, he bent towards her and whispered, 'Please, Jill. Please come back to me.' Brushing her hair out of her eyes he continued, 'I love you and we have such a wonderful future ahead of us. Please, darling, wake up and say you'll marry me and be my wife.' He kissed her tenderly on the lips.

Looking up he saw Byrd and Jo embracing, lost in their own love for each other. He so desperately wanted that for himself and Jill. Then he felt movement. Jill was stirring, coming round, and struggling to get up. Thanking God and praising his name, Osian soothed her and help her sit up. 'Just take a few minutes, darling, you're going to be fine,' he said with conviction as he committed their future into God's hands.

As Jill and Osian sat looking out to sea, there was no sign of the Kelpie.

CHAPTER 49

Jo savoured Eddie's touch. He was freezing and wet through, but neither of them cared, the only thing on their minds was that the Kelpie was dead, and they were both alive.

'That was such a bloody stupid thing to do, Byrd,' she said. 'Going after Jill like that.'

'Oh, so I should have let her die, should I?'

'She wouldn't have died. The Kelpie didn't want her, she captured young men, remember? Young men like you. She could have gone after you.'

'But she didn't.'

'No, I know. But how often do you hear tales of dogs being in danger of drowning, so their owners swim out to save them and they end up dead, but the dogs survive. I mean, honestly, Byrd, I was so scared.'

'About what?'

'That you wouldn't come out of the sea. That you'd die.'

'Don't be soft,' he said pushing her hair behind her ear. 'I'll never die!' he finished with a flourish.

'Ha, so you'll live forever then?' she teased.

'I'll live for as long as you love me.'

That stopped Jo in her tracks. 'Love you?'

'Yes, if you love me like I love you.'

A stunned Jo was trying to think of a suitable response when Osian shouted, 'Look there, floating in the water.'

Their moment lost, Jo and Byrd followed Osian's finger. There was something being washed ashore. It looked like a tangle of rope. A wave dropped it at Osian's feet. Picking it up he exclaimed, 'It's a bridle. The Kelpie's bridle.'

Jo smiled. 'You did it Osian, you really did it.'

'No, we all did it. We all believed. We all defeated it.'

The relief made Jo buckle at the knees. The Kelpie was really gone and would take no more young men. But where the hell were the victims? Where were the 10 missing men? Could they have got it completely wrong? Was it not the Kelpie taking them at all, but some other entity? There was no doubt they'd killed the Kelpie. But now Jo began to doubt that the Kelpie was responsible. Judith had assured Jo the men would be returned if the Kelpie was killed. But there was no sign of them. No one else except their wet and totally exhausted ragged band of brothers. She turned away from the sea, dispirited, convinced they'd failed.

CHAPTER 50

Jo turned away from the sea to walk back to her car. All she wanted was to stop shivering, take off her wet coat and towel dry her hair. She was intending to put the heating on full blast.

'I don't believe it,' muttered Byrd.

Jo stopped. 'Believe what?'

'Isn't that Judith? But she looks a bit hazy. What do you reckon?'

Jo turned around to see what Byrd was talking about, and there was Judith walking out of the sea towards them. Byrd was right, she did seem more like a mirage than a person. Or should that be like a ghost? Jo didn't know much of anything anymore. She was confused by the whole evening. As Judith paddled in the shallows, Jo could see that following her out of the sea came the lost young men. Somehow Judith had found them and led them here.

'Bloody hell,' said Byrd.

'Thank God,' said Osian.

Jill burst out crying.

'Are they real? Or are they ghosts like you?' Jo asked Judith.

To which Judith smiled that enigmatic smile of hers, which meant she wasn't going to dignify that question with an answer. Even though the release of the 10 was the outcome they had all hoped for, at the same time it was totally unexpected.

Judith said, 'They have been released from their watery jails where they were held by the magic of the Kelpie in underground chambers.'

As the men stumbled out of the sea, Osian and Jill went to them, helping them out of the water and leading them to the top of the beach.

10 young men. Lost for three years. Now found. Each of their names etched in her heart.

Jo swallowed the lump in her throat and plucked her mobile out of her pocket. They needed help. Ambulances. And Jo needed officers to do preliminary interviews and to contact relatives. Calls made, she followed Byrd to the promenade where the men were milling around. Dazed.

Jill came up to Jo and said, 'They don't seem to know where they are or where they've been.'

Jo figured that was understandable, they'd suffered a severe trauma.

Byrd walked up to the two women. 'Have you noticed? They are dry! I expected them to be wet through coming from the sea.'

Jo quickly came to a decision and called Osian over. 'Byrd has pointed out that our victims are dry. We can't have them stumbling out of the sea, dry!'

'So what do we say?'

'They wandered along the beach. We're not sure where they've come from, maybe caves?'

'From caves?' said Byrd. 'Seriously?'

'Well that would explain why they're not wet through,' said Jill. 'But where are the caves?'

'I don't bloody know, but it's better than everyone thinking there was something supernatural about the whole thing. No one else knows about the Kelpie apart from us four. So no one else needs to know that the men stumbled out of the sea but are inexplicably dry!'

'They'll know,' Byrd said, pointing to the men.

'I doubt it,' said Osian. 'The poor victims hardly know who they are, never mind where they are and where they've been. If everybody talks about them being held in caves, they'll soon believe it themselves.'

CHAPTER 51

Jo looked along the seafront of Pagham. The road running
at the top of the beach was now filled with vehicles,
mostly ambulances. But there were also marked police
cars, parked at either end of the line, making sure the road
stayed closed while the emergency services worked. Sat
on the back steps of ambulances, colour seemed to be
returning to the young men's faces. They had all been as
pale as Judith when they first appeared, prompting Jo to
be afraid that they were dead, and she'd just saved ghostly
apparitions. According to the paramedics, most victims
seemed exhausted, dehydrated, malnourished and very
confused. They had no idea where they'd been, or how
long they'd been gone. But no one pushed them for
memories or explanations, there would be plenty of time
for that in the days and weeks to come. For now it was
enough that they were still alive and would be returning
to their families very soon.

Taking a moment, Jo was looking out to sea on her
own. After the mad panic of the appearance of the victims
and then sirens that split the night with their raucous
wailings and flashing lights, all was calm. The
experienced professionals taking over from Jo and her

crew. She would be able to interview the young men in the coming days, for now she'd leave them to their families.

A flash of colour against the dark glass of the swollen sea caught Jo's eye. The tide had turned and there was something riding the incoming waves. As it drew nearer, Jo walked to the edge of the sea and began to see the outline of a body. A female body. Floating just out of reach. Without thought for her safety, she waded into the sea.

Byrd must have seen her go for she heard his shouts floating over the beach to her.

'Jo, for God's sake, come back!' As he ran nearer, she could hear him say, 'Don't, don't, come back, you don't know what it is!'

He was pleading with her, but she ignored his warnings.

'It could be a ploy. A decoy. The Kelpie. Anything. It's too dangerous, come back!'

It seemed Byrd was afraid he'd never see her again, but Jo couldn't stop. She had to find out who was floating in on the tide. The Kelpie? Or another victim they'd not heard of? Whoever it was, it was Jo's responsibility to find out. For otherwise this night would never end. There would always be the threat from the Kelpie in the background of their lives. Burrowing into their dreams. Turning them from benign stories into nightmares, frightening in their intensity. No, she had to complete the mission, otherwise their lives would be forever blighted by the legend of the Kelpie.

In the end, Jo didn't have to go far into the sea to claim her prize. The body seemed to float straight into her hands. Scooping it up in her arms, Jo turned and staggered out of the water. It was the body of a young woman, pale and beautiful, with flowers wound in her long damp ringlets.

'This time we have a villain!' she called triumphantly. 'And Sykes can't do a damn thing to us!'

CHAPTER 52

The following morning, Jo and Byrd passed the scrum of reporters camping out, opposite the entrance to Chichester Hospital. For once the press loved them. The police were heroes. They'd found the missing men all alive and well. The only fatality, the body of a young woman who had yet to be identified. But, of course, there were the inevitable questions:

'Were they all kept prisoner together?'

'Why?'

'By whom?'

'Where were they kept?'

'Detective Inspector can you comment on the investigations at all?'

'When will there be a press conference?'

They shouted questions that Jo and Byrd didn't really have answers to. This was their first chance to speak to the men, to try to find out what had happened. Last night the doctors had refused to let the police interview anyone and they were all banned from the ward until tests were completed and any treatment regime implemented. Most were severely dehydrated and under nourished.

Upon reaching the relative calm inside, Jo and Byrd

went in the lift to a private ward, Jo with her heart in her mouth all the way up. It was on the sixth floor and Byrd had refused to climb up all those steps. Stumbling out of the lift, they were let into the ward by the duty policemen, who inspected their credentials and made them sign in, even though he knew full well who they were. Jo was reassured by that. There was also a list of permitted visitors. No one else would get near the men and one of their biggest officers had been especially chosen for the job.

Pushing through the door, they quickly found out which room Colin was in and Byrd tapped on the door before entering. Colin was lying on top of the bed, dressed in pyjamas and dressing gown. He was alone.

'Hi, Colin,' said Jo. 'Is it alright to come in and speak to you?' Colin nodded and as they walked up to the bed she continued, 'On your own? No mum and dad?'

'They've gone home for a bit, to eat something and change their clothes, maybe even have a few hours' sleep.'

'Of course,' Jo said. 'They must have been here all night.'

Colin nodded.

'Can you tell us the last thing you remember?' asked Byrd.

'I remember kissing a beautiful girl on the edge of the lagoon and then nothing until you found me on the beach.'

'What about the others? The other men? Do you remember them?'

'No. I thought I was alone until I saw them on the beach.'

Jo was horrified to see Colin's eyes fill with tears. She pulled up a chair to the side of the bed. His hand was trembling, and he was losing the fight with the urge to cry. She grabbed his hand. 'It's alright, Colin. You're safe now.'

As he nodded, the hospital bed disappeared. In its place was an ornate metal one. There were muslin drapes all around the room, although Jo couldn't see any windows, and soft lighting. There as a damp, musty smell and Jo could hear the sound of dripping water. There was a chill in the air that had nothing to do with the temperature and everything to do with the cold fear that was spreading down Jo's spine. Dancing and cavorting around the room was a beautiful young woman with dark ringlets intertwined with flowers.

'Don't you find me beautiful?' she cooed.

Jo looked back at the bed, where Colin was lying. He was tethered to the bed by a leather rein that connected to the bridle he wore. It was wrapped around his face and head, with a bit pulled painfully tight in his mouth. Dully he dutifully nodded.

'What? I can't hear you, Colin.'

'Yes,' he mumbled.

'Louder.'

'Yes.'

'Louder!'

'Yes, yes, alright,' he shouted.

Jo watched in horror as he pulled at the bridle, trying to yank it off his face. But there were no buckles to undo. No clips to unclasp. It was stuck to his face as though with superglue. Tears rolled down his face and Jo's heart ached for him.

'Why do you have to be so hurtful?' the girl said. 'You know what happens when you're hurtful, don't you?'

Colin looked at her, resignation written all over his face. Jo watched in horror as the girl grabbed a riding crop off the bed.

'This is what happens.'

The crop cracked against Colin's legs.

'Tell me you love me,' she demanded and flexed the whip in front of his face.

Colin just looked at her. His punishment was a whipped chest.

'Tell me you love me,' she demanded again.

This time Colin succumbed. 'I love you,' he whispered. 'I want to stay with you forever. I never want to leave you.'

'There,' the Kelpie smiled. 'That wasn't so hard, was it?'

Jo closed her eyes. She couldn't look any more.

When she opened them, she was back in the hospital room.

'I'm sorry I can't remember,' Colin was saying. 'I'm sorry I can't help.'

Jo nodded. 'It's alright, we understand. Don't worry. Why don't we see if we can rustle up a nice cuppa for you?'

Colin nodded and she left the room with Byrd. Once outside Jo sagged against the wall.

'That bad?' asked Byrd.

'Worse,' she said and walked away from the tortured man in the hospital room. 'Mind you, there's still one thing hanging above Colin's head and that's the girls he raped before he was taken by the Kelpie. Even if he can't remember the terrible way he treated them, they can and don't forget it's all documented in his diary. So if even one of them decides to press charges....'

Jo left the rest unsaid as her mobile rang. Answering the call, she saw it was from Del Deed.

'Good morning, Mr Deed,' she said.

'Morning, DI Wolfe. I just wanted to thank you...' the hesitant voice fell silent.

'No thanks needed, Mr Deed. I was just doing my job,' she said. 'We're all glad the case was brought to a successful conclusion.'

'Yes, yes.' Once again, Del fell silent.

'I appreciate the call, Mr Deed, but - '

'Yes, of course, you must be very busy. Please thank your officers for me,' he said and rang off.

Jo had the feeling that that was a very hard call for Del Deed to make, after the accusations the Deed's had made about the lack of progress and the awful mistakes that had been made during the investigation. Jo allowed herself a small smile, then looked up as Jill came down the corridor towards them.

'Oh, hi, Boss.'

'Morning, Jill. So, what's the current position?'

'Well, as we thought last night, all are suffering from dehydration and are painfully thin. The men that have been lost the longest are the worst, up to Colin there, who was the last to go missing. He's faring better than the others, but not by much. They are all suffering from retrograde amnesia. The doctors have confirmed it's not unusual in cases like this, for the victims to have no memories of their captor or their time in captivity. The mind shuts down to protect itself from the horrors it's experienced.'

'How long will it last?'

'Apparently you can never tell. Sometimes a few short weeks or months, in rare cases years or even never,' Jill explained.

Byrd said, 'Best not to push them to remember, don't you think?'

Jo agreed with him. 100%. The thought of the men telling tales of being held hostage by a supernatural being, under the sea, filled Jo with dread. She fervently hoped they'd never remember. Ever.

CHAPER 53

Later that day, back at the station, Sykes demanded that Jo meet him in his office. She ran up the stairs, case folder in hand, hopeful that, for once, she'd get praise instead of criticism.

She knocked on Sykes' open door and he called her in. She sat in the low visitor's chair, folder on her lap, looking at him expectantly.

'Oh, dear, dear, dear, Jo,' he said. 'Well, once again you've not got the perpetrator of these terrible crimes.'

She was stunned. But then again, had she really expected Sykes to have changed?

'But, Sir, the young woman…'

He cut her off. 'There's no evidence that she was holding them against their will. None of them have the faintest idea where they were held, or why, or by whom.'

'But the men have identified her as the last person they can remember meeting.' Jo couldn't believe what she was hearing.

'But how do we know that? Where were they? It's rather convenient for you that they don't know or can't remember because of the trauma. Can any of them take us to where they were held?'

Sykes held up a restraining hand as Jo went to speak again.

'We need a crime scene and you haven't provided one. Nor have you provided a reasonable explanation as to what happened to them. So, I'm going to recommend an enquiry into your cases. Until then you're suspended.'

'But….'

'Jo this is not up for discussion.' He held out his hand. 'Warrant card and pass please.'

Distraught, Jo stumbled into her office. Thankfully, the team were all still at the hospital, so no one was there to witness her shame. Suspended! Like some wet behind the ears cop who had made an almighty cock-up. Grabbing her bag, shoes, and phone, she left the station as fast as she could, not even stopping to chat to Jed on her way out.

As she drove home, she rang Byrd to tell him of her predicament. His reaction was as expected. He'd meet her at the flat as soon as he could, then they could talk strategy. But the only strategy Jo could come up with, was to tell her dad. In her heart she knew that this was a typical Sykes power play; quick to jump on any perceived infringement by her or her team. At least this time his venom was directed at her and not them. It was nothing to do with Byrd, Jill, Ken and Sasha, and everything to do with Sykes hating her and her father, Mick.

Pulling up on the gravel drive outside their home, Jo stumbled out of the car and up the steps of the main house, where her father was already waiting.

'I've just spoken to Byrd,' he said and opened his arms.

Jo fell into them and let go of the tight reins holding her emotions in check. After her storm of tears had abated, he led her into the kitchen where Honey and freshly brewed coffee were waiting. The two comforts of family life.

CHAPTER 54

In the end the strategy was simple. Mick invited the Chief Supt over that evening. Accepting a glass of wine (his driver was waiting with the car outside), Jo's boss' boss, settled into the comfortable leather armchair and took a long drink.

'Very nice, thanks, Mick. Right,' he turned his attention to Jo and Byrd. 'I'm here to find out, informally, what's been going on. But first of all, what is this vendetta all about, Mick? Between you and Sykes?'

Mick sighed. 'It was years ago.'

'And?'

'Sykes messed up on a murder investigation we were working on together. We were both green, wet behind the ears, detective constables, and this case was to be our big break. But Sykes made a monumental mistake in procedure. He was supposed to collect background information on a man who wasn't in the frame for the murder, or anything like that. At that time he was merely a possible person of interest.

'The upshot was that Sykes didn't do the background checks, but pretended he had, and said that there was nothing to be concerned about there. Later, when it became clear that the man Sykes had failed to look into was likely their killer and yet another young woman had lost her life, Sykes asked me to cover for him. To say that Sykes had done the work and that I had seen the background checks.

'Well, of course, I refused and when interviewed by the Detective Chief Inspector leading the case, I told him I knew what Sykes had done. Sykes got severely reprimanded and pushed back down into uniform as a community support officer. From that day on Sykes has hated me. And then transferred that hatred to Jo, as he saw an opportunity to hurt me, but this time through her.'

The Chief Supt nodded and took another drink. 'OK, that explains Sykes. Now explain the cases to me, for hate him or not, the DCI does have a point, Jo. I want to know precisely what had happened in your last four cases, including this one. And who was the perpetrator in each case and why he or she is not in custody.'

Jo looked at Byrd, who grabbed her hand and said, 'Go on. Tell him. It worked for me, understanding what was going on. The Chief deserves the truth.'

And so, starting with Jo's accident and the gift she'd brought back with her from being in a coma, they told the Chief the truth, from the case of Anubis, the God of Death, all the way up to the Kelpie and what Jo had seen when she'd 'read' Colin.

Even Mick was taken aback by the depth of some of the horrors they'd seen and evil entities they'd had to battle. His hand shook as he poured more wine.

'Let me think on this overnight,' the Chief said. 'Be in the conference room at 10 am tomorrow, both of you. Oh and you better get Jill and Father Price there as well. No buts or maybes. Be there.'

CHAPTER 55

The following morning, the four friends met in the conference room at Chichester Police Station. It was just before 10 am and all were extremely nervous. Jill, Byrd, and Jo didn't want to lose their jobs and Osian felt as though all of this was his fault. He wasn't quite sure how, but was happy to take the blame anyway, for anything, just to save them.

A tall man opened the door. He was dressed in a pristine white shirt with epaulets on it, which was paired with trousers with the sharpest crease Osian had ever seen. The man had the presence of a leader. It could only be the Chief Superintendent. His three friends jumped to their feet, so he followed their lead.

'Sit, sit,' was the order, with the wave of a hand, so they did and the Chief Supt sat at the head of the table.

Osian saw Jo's hand was shaking and her face was white. Byrd openly held her hand and gave a small smile of encouragement. Osian took Byrd's lead and held Jill's hand, but under the table. Her knuckles were white as she gripped his hand tightly, to the point of being painful, but he handled the pain stoically.

He looked around at their small band of brothers. The

three talented police officers, so brave in the face of evil. Surely this man would understand what they'd done and why they'd done it?

'Well,' the Chief Superintendent looked at each one of them in turn. 'What's to be done with you lot?'

Osian went to speak, but Jill kicked him on the ankle, and he grimaced with pain, but shut his mouth.

'I've decided...' the Chief paused dramatically and Osian rather felt that the Sword of Damocles' was hanging over their collective heads, 'to do nothing.'

The four looked at each other in surprise. 'Nothing, Sir?' said Jo.

'That's right, nothing. You are all to carry on as normal, but I don't want the details of your escapades being talked about in the police station. This will be our secret. When you take another case, you will work directly under my supervision. Got it?'

They all nodded enthusiastically.

'I'm sure we can find lots of strange, weird and wonderful cases for you all to get to the bottom of. I'll assign the cases, but in the meantime carry on with closing down the missing men case.'

They rose as the Chief left and then fell back into their chairs.

Byrd exhaled. 'Phew, that's a result, don't you think?'

Jo nodded. 'Yes, thank goodness. I was truly afraid we'd gone too far and were about to lose our jobs.'

Jill rose, 'So back to work everyone?'

'Hang on a minute,' said Jo, looking at Jill's left hand. 'What's that you've got on your finger?'

Osian's good mood evaporated and once more he was filled with anxiety and doubt. His name really should be Thomas, he was sure of it.

'Osian asked me to marry him last night,' Jill flapped her left hand at Jo. 'And clearly I accepted!'

'Oh, that's wonderful news,' and Jo walked round to

Jill and gave her a big hug, as Byrd shook Osian's hand.

'I'm so happy for you both. But I'm afraid we have work to do, so let's get on with it and celebrate tonight. Dinner on us,' she looked at Byrd who nodded his agreement.

Osian was relieved. Jo and Byrd were not just Jill's colleagues, but her closest friends and he'd hoped they would approve of their union. He was looking forward to an evening out and for all four of them to let their hair down, after what they'd been through in the past few weeks. He still couldn't believe he'd taken the shot and killed the Kelpie. It was an extra-ordinary thing to have done, for such an ordinary cleric.

Later that evening, Jo and Byrd were getting ready to go out to dinner with Jill and Osian. 'I'm so happy for them,' said Jo, putting on a pair of earrings.

'Mmm, me too,' said Byrd. 'Um, what do you reckon?'

Byrd was standing behind her so Jo looked at his reflection in the bedroom mirror. 'What do you mean?'

'About us. Putting things on a more permanent footing.'

'You mean marriage? Us?'

Byrd quickly shook his head. 'No, but definitely living together. What do you think?' he moved closer, wrapping his arms around her from behind and nuzzling her neck.

Jo turned in his arms. 'I think we're quite different to Jill and Osian. They are both believers and because of their faith, they'd want to do things the right way in their minds. Firstly getting engaged, then married and finally living together. I get the feeling they're rather old-fashioned like that. But,' Jo snaked her arms around Byrd's neck, 'I'd love for you to be around all the time. I think we are both lonely living on our own and we spend much of our time together anyway. So why not?'

Byrd's answer was a long, lingering kiss, which was broken by the sound of Mick clomping up the stairs.

'Ha,' he said, a little out of breath. 'Sorry to disturb and all that.'

Jo turned to her father, beaming. 'Byrd here has just asked me to live with him.'

'Have I?'

'Well, not in so many words, but yes.'

Byrd grinned. 'OK, I'll go along with that.'

'Too bloody right,' said Mick. 'Look, I suspected as much, so I've a little gift for you.'

'A gift,' Jo stepped back from Eddie. 'What kind of gift.'

'This kind,' and opening his hand Mick revealed an ornate key.

'What's that?' asked Byrd.

'The key to the house,' said Jo dropping onto the bed.

'It's time we swapped living spaces, don't you think? This flat's too small for the two of you to live in permanently and it's just the right size for me and Honey. And we can still use the main house when the family descend on us.'

At the sound of her name, Honey came bounding up the stairs and bowled into the bedroom. She immediately jumped on the bed, turned around a few times, then settled down and went to sleep.

'See, Honey's made it her home already!'

CHAPTER 56

'Morning, Jed,' said Jo, as she entered the station, her position duly restored by the Chief.

'Morning, Guv. Heard the news?' Jed was a constant source of station gossip, but it was usually right. 'Our friend DCI Sykes has been moved on.'

'Really? Are you sure?' Relief made Jo's legs weak, and she grabbed hold of the counter.

'Positive, as he's been taken off the On-Call rota and his cases passed to a temporary replacement.'

'How do you know?'

'Because here at the front desk I have to know who's doing what so I can deal with members of the public and help direct them to the correct officer,' he said rather pompously.

Jo grinned. 'Of course you do. Where's he gone?'

'Rumour has it, back up to Yorkshire. Miserable git deserves everything he gets. Anyway I take it all went well with the meeting with the Chief and your friends yesterday,' Jed said with a twinkle in his eye.

'How do you know...' but of course Jed knew. There wasn't much that went on in the station that he didn't know about.

'They make a lovely couple, don't you think? Our Jill and that Father Price?'

'Yes, yes, I do, Jed. Let's hope she'll be happy with him.'

'Oh I think so. She deserves happiness.'

'Yes, yes, she does. Anyway, must press on, Jed. Places to go, people to see.'

'Stay safe, Jo.'

'Always, Jed, always.'

Playing with the Dead

Young people are dying after playing the same video game in an empty bedroom. YOU'RE DEAD blinking on and off on the screen.

Foretelling doom? The end of the game? Or the end of the player?

Soon he's not the only victim.

The parents believe it must be their fault. They never should have let their children play such an awful game. But no one could have known how violent the games were. Or had never bothered to find out.

Their children had played the game for far too long, sometimes all night, sometimes for days on end.

Causing DI Jo Wolfe to wonder if the children were obsessed, or possessed?

Coming in January 2021!
Available on pre-order from your local Amazon store.

By Wendy Cartmell

Sgt Major Crane crime thrillers:
Deadly Steps
Deadly Nights
Deadly Honour
Deadly Lies
Deadly Hijack
Deadly Widow
Deadly Cut
Deadly Proof

Crane and Anderson crime thrillers:
Death Rites
Death Elements
Death Call
A Grave Death
A Cold Death

Emma Harrison mysteries
Past Judgement
Mortal Judgement
Joint Judgement

Supernatural suspense
Gamble with Death
Touching the Dead
Divining the Dead
Watching the Dead
Waking the Dead
Playing with the Dead

All my books are in KINDLE UNLIMITED and
available to purchase or borrow from Amazon.

Check out my website and blog, where I review the very best in crime fiction.

wendycartmell.com

Happy reading
until next time…

Printed in Great Britain
by Amazon

27321733R00101